PRAISE FOR *Homeless Bird*

"Graceful and evocative."
—*The New York Times Book Review*

"Whelan has entered into an imagined world with empathy and riveting authenticity."
—*The Boston Sunday Globe*

"Kids will likely enjoy [the] dramatic view of an endangered adolescence and cheer Koly's hard-won victories."
—*Publishers Weekly*

"An insightful, beautifully written, culturally illuminating tale."
—ALA *Booklist* (starred review)

"Whelan's writing is lyrical and filled with evocative images. This diminutive book delivers a mighty wallop."
—*San Francisco Examiner & Chronicle*

"Believable and satisfying." —*Riverbank Review*

"Whelan embroiders details and traditions into an artful contemporary novel that is as textured and seamless as her heroine's needlework." —*School Library Journal*

"Beautifully written. Koly is a memorable heroine readers will care about and love." —*The Book Report* (starred review)

"*Homeless Bird* is dazzling from cover to cover." —*The Five Owls*

"Vividly realized." —*Kirkus Reviews* (pointer review)

A National Book Award Winner • An ALA Notable Book
An ALA Best Book for Young Adults
A *School Library Journal* Best Book
ALA *Booklist*'s Book for Youth Editor's Choice
International Reading Association Notable Book for a Global Socety

Homeless Bird

Gloria Whelan

HARPERTROPHY®
An Imprint of HarperCollins*Publishers*

Harper Trophy® is a registered trademark of
HarperCollins Publishers Inc.

Homeless Bird

Library of Congress Cataloging-in-Publication Data
Whelan, Gloria.

Homeless bird / Gloria Whelan.

   p.   cm.

   Summary: When thirteen-year old Koly enters into an ill-fated
arranged marriage, she must either suffrer a destiny dictated by
India's tradition or find the courage to oppose it.

   ISBN 0-06-028454-4. — ISBN 0-06-028452-8 (lib. bdg.)

   ISBN 0-06-440819-1 (pbk.)

   [1. Courage—Fiction. 2. India—Fiction.] I. Title.

PZ7.W5718Ho 2000   99-33241

[Fic]—dc21   CIP

                                AC

Typography by Alison Donalty

❖ First Harper Trophy edition, 2001

Visit us on the World Wide Web! www.harperchildrens.com

10 11 12 13 LP/CW 30 29 28 27 26 25

for Jacqueline and Patrick

o n e

"Koly, you are thirteen and growing every day,"
Maa said to me. "It's time for you to have a husband." I knew why. There were days when my maa
took only a bit of rice for herself so that the rest of
us—my baap, my brothers, and I—might have
more. "It's one of my days to fast," she would say,
as if it were a holy thing, but I knew it was because
there was not enough food to go around. The day I
left home, there would be a little more for everyone
else. I had known the day was coming, but the
regret I saw in Maa's eyes made me tremble.

My baap, like all fathers with a daughter to
marry off, had to find a dowry for me. "It will be
no easy task," he said with a sigh. Baap was a

scribe. He sat all day in his marketplace stall hoping to make a few rupees by writing letters for those who did not know how to write their own. His customers had little money. Often from the goodness of his heart Baap would write the letter for only a rupee or two. When I was a small girl, he would sometimes let me stand beside him. I watched as the spoken words were written down to become like caged birds, caught forever by my clever baap.

When they learned Maa and Baap were looking for a husband for me, my two brothers began to tease me. My older brother, Gopal, said, "Koly, when you have a husband, you will have to do as he tells you. You won't sit and daydream as you do now."

My younger brother, Ram, whom I always beat at card games, said, "When you play cards with your husband, you'll have to lose every time."

My brothers went to the boys' school in our village. Though there was a school for girls, I did not go there. I had begged to go, promising I would get up early and stay up late to do my work, but Maa said school was a waste for girls. "It will be of no use to you after you are married. The money for books and school fees is better put toward your dowry, so that we may find you a suitable husband."

When I stole looks into my brothers' books, I saw secrets in the characters I could not puzzle out. When I begged them to teach me the secrets, they laughed at me. Gopal complained, "I have to sit in a hot schoolroom all day and have my knuckles rapped if I look out the window. You are the lucky one."

Ram said, "When a girl learns to read, her hair falls out, her eyes cross, and no man will look at her."

Still, I turned over the pages of my brothers' books. When Maa sent me into the village for some errand, I lingered under the windows of the school to listen to the students saying their lessons aloud. But the lessons were not like measles. I did not catch them.

My maa had no use for books. When she was not taking care of the house, she spent her time embroidering. Like her maa before her, and her maa, and as far back as anyone could remember, the women in our family embroidered. All their thoughts and dreams went into their work. Maa embroidered the borders for saris sold in our marketplace. One sari might take many weeks, for a sari stretched all the way across the room. Because it took so long, each sari became a part of our lives. As soon as I could work with a needle, I was allowed to stitch simple designs. As I grew older, Maa gave me peacocks and ducks to embroider. When the border was finished, Maa took the sari to the marketplace. Then there would be rupees to spare in the house.

Now Maa sat with a length of red muslin for my wedding sari on her lap. Because he valued her work, the shopkeeper had sold the sari to Maa for a good price. She was embroidering a border of lotus flowers, a proper border for a wedding sari, because the lotus pod's many seeds are scattered to the wind, suggesting wealth and plenty.

Relatives and friends began to search for a bridegroom. A part of me hoped they would be successful and that someone wanted me. A part of me hoped that no one in the world would want me enough to take me away from my home and my maa and baap and brothers. I knew that after my marriage, I would have to make my home with the family of my husband. For my dowry I began to embroider a quilt, making all my worries stitches, and all the things I would have to leave behind pictures to take with me.

I embroidered my maa in her green sari and my baap on the bicycle that took him to the marketplace every morning. My brothers played at soccer with a ball they had fashioned from old rags. I added the feathery leaves of the tamarind tree that stood in the middle of our courtyard and our cow under its shade. I put in the sun that beat down on the courtyard and the clouds that gathered before the rains. I put myself at the courtyard well, where I was sent many times each day to get water. I stitched the marketplace stalls heaped with turmeric and cinnamon and cumin and mustard. I embroidered vegetable stalls with purple eggplants and green melons. I made the barber cutting hair, the dentist pulling teeth, the man who cleaned ears, and the man with the basket of cobras. Because I was kept busy at all my other tasks, the stitching took many weeks.

While I stitched, I wondered what my husband would be like. Stories were told of girls having to marry old men, but I did not think Maa and Baap would let that happen to me. In my daydreams I hoped for someone who was handsome and who would be kind to me.

My older brother said, "We're too poor to buy you a decent husband."

My younger brother said, "There is sure to be something wrong with anyone who agrees to marry you."

When I heard that at last a husband had been found for me, I almost ran away. How could I spend the rest of my days with someone I had never seen? Yet Maa had finished embroidering the wedding sari, Baap had written a letter of acceptance to the bridegroom's family, and my brothers began to treat me with respect, so I didn't run away.

A gift of money had to be paid to my bridegroom's family for taking me. To get money for the dowry, Maa sold three brass vases and a brass wedding lamp that had been a part of her own dowry. Hardest of all, our cow had to go. The family would no longer have fresh, rich milk to churn for butter to make into ghee. Instead they would have to buy ghee in the marketplace, where it was expensive and not fresh. Money was not enough, though. The family of my bridegroom asked, "What jewelry will she bring?"

I had two bangles made of glass beads and some plastic toe rings, nothing more. I heard Maa and Baap talking together so late in the night that the moon slid up and down in the sky. The next morning Maa brought out the silver earrings she had worn as a bride. They were solid silver, and so heavy that when I tried them on, I was afraid my ears would stretch to the size of an elephant's. The bridegroom's family was satisfied.

To please me, my baap asked for my bridegroom's picture, but none was sent. I knew little about him except that his name was Hari Mehta and that he was sixteen. "He has a younger sister," Maa said, "so you will have help with the household tasks."

The marriage was considered a good one. Hari's baap, like mine, was a Brahman, the highest Hindu caste, and he was a schoolteacher. Hari would surely have been to school. "Will he mind that I have no learning?" I wondered aloud.

"What do you mean no learning?" Maa asked in a cross voice. "You can cook and keep a house, and you embroider as well as I do. Should a wife sit with a book and let the work go?"

Even though it meant leaving my home for the home of my bridegroom's family, I was becoming very nearly happy about my wedding. There was someone who wanted me. Best of all, instead of scraps from my maa's worn saris, I was to have a sari of my own to wear.

Because the Mehtas were anxious to have the ceremony as soon as possible, the astrologer was told to be quick in fixing an auspicious date for the wedding. The ceremony was to take place at Hari's home instead of our home. This was not usual, but it pleased my parents, for it meant they would not have the expense of feeding wedding guests.

My brothers were not to come with us. I dared to hug them as I said good-bye. My older brother looked embarrassed, and my younger one shy, as I clung to them. Though they sometimes teased and tricked me, they could be kind as well. If no one was around to see him, my older brother would help me carry the heavy pails of mud from the pond to plaster our walls. My younger brother had once caught four fireflies in a jar for me.

As I walked out of the courtyard with Maa and Baap, I looked back. The courtyard was where we had our meals and where we slept on warm nights. I would awaken to the sound of the cuckoo in the tamarind tree that shaded the courtyard. Maa and I would wash our hair by the courtyard well and dry it in the sun. Then we would braid each other's hair. Once when the small wild lilies were blooming, I wove them into Maa's hair, and she laughed like a girl. All this I was leaving behind.

I carried with me my quilt, a sandalwood box that held the silver earrings, and a photograph of my parents, my two brothers, and myself. It had been taken the year before by a traveling photographer. My brothers and I are grinning, but my maa looks angry and my baap guilty. I remember maa saying the five rupees the picture cost would have bought half a kilo of rice. At first the colors of the picture had been too showy and not as they were in real life, but after a year they faded into softer, lifelike colors.

I felt tears stinging my eyes as the bus pulled out of the station. It would take me to the Mehtas' village, but it would not bring me back. Maa must have had the same thought; she reached for my hand and held it tightly.

Mr. Mehta was there when the bus stopped. He was a short man with a small round face and a pair of large, dark-rimmed glasses. It was hard to see his face behind the glasses. I made my best ceremonial namaskar, saluting him and even touching his feet, but he gave me only a quick look. Instead he turned to Baap and, after a courteous but quick greeting, asked, "You have brought the dowry, sir?" Until that moment I had believed it was me the Mehta family wanted; now it seemed that what they cared for most was the dowry. Was my marriage to be like the buying of a sack of yams in the market-place?

A wagon drawn by two bullocks took us down a dusty road. The hot winds sent the bamboo groves rustling. Even the crows seemed restless, lighting on first one tree and then another as if the branches were hot to the touch. I heard Maa whisper that we should have been met with something better than a wagon, but we soon saw that the distance to the Mehtas' home was not far.

The Mehtas' house was larger than ours, but some of the mud-brick walls were tumbled, and a part of the house had no roof. A scrawny cow, look-ing like a pile of bones, was slumped down in the middle of the courtyard. We were greeted by evil-tempered geese hissing at us. Mr. Mehta shooed them away and led us to the doorway, where Mrs.

Mehta met us. She was tall and shadow thin, with small bright bird eyes and a sharp nose. I bowed and touched her feet. Unlike her husband, she looked closely at me. I was conscious of my unruly hair that would not be trapped in a neat braid and my enormous eyes, which my younger brother called owl eyes. As always when I met someone new, I didn't know what to do with my hands and feet.

"Your girl is big for her age," Mrs. Mehta said to Maa. "That's good. There is plenty for her to do here."

"Koly is a good worker," Maa replied. There was pride in her voice, but I saw that something was bothering her. I was beginning to wish I were back home. I had not expected to be made much of, but so far there was little welcome in the Mehtas' greeting.

A girl who looked a year or so younger than me was staring at us from a corner of the room. "Chandra," Mrs. Mehta called, "come here and meet your new sister-in-law."

Chandra was very beautiful, with golden-brown

skin and sad, pleading eyes. She was plump, with a soft round face and body. Her thick black hair hung loosely over her shoulders, partly covering her face. She bowed shyly to me and then looked quickly away, as if she knew secrets about me that I did not.

Mrs. Mehta prodded her husband, giving him a sharp glance. Looking embarrassed, Mr. Mehta beckoned to Baap saying, "There are one or two things to settle before the wedding."

Mrs. Mehta showed Maa and me to a room inside the house. As soon as she left us, I whispered, "When will I see Hari?"

Maa said, "Tomorrow at the wedding ceremony. Before would not be proper."

"What if I don't like him?"

"Of course you will like him."

"But what if I don't?"

Maa impatiently slapped at a fly. "Then you must learn to like him." She put her arms around me, and I felt the wetness of her tears against my cheek. I began to cry as well.

There was only a curtain between my rope cot and the charpoy of my parents. When Baap returned, I heard him say to Maa, "He has the money now, and soon he will have our daughter."

"Did you see the son?" Maa asked.

"No. Mehta said the boy has a bit of flu and is resting for the ceremonies tomorrow."

"That is not auspicious," Maa said.

"Nothing here is auspicious," Baap replied.

In a frightened voice Maa asked, "Should we postpone the wedding?"

Baap's voice was hard. "Don't even speak of such a thing! You know if a wedding does not take place at the appointed time, some evil is sure to come to the bride."

Too frightened by their words to sleep, I lay awake that night listening to the unfamiliar sounds. Voices rose and fell in a nearby room, and from another direction someone coughed. I longed to beg my parents to take me home. I would promise to eat very little and work very hard. But I could not ask such a thing. To refuse to go through with the marriage would bring dishonor on my family. I told myself that if my eyes were not so big or my nose smaller, if I were not so large or my hair straighter, the Mehtas would be kinder. Still I knew that despite my flaws, my parents cared for me. Perhaps, I comforted myself, in time the Mehtas would too. Or if they didn't grow to like me, they would at least get used to me.

Maa got me up so early, the pigeons had not yet begun their cooing. We went to the courtyard well and drew water to wash my hair. Maa oiled and braided it. She dusted my face with golden turmeric powder, and with a paste of sandalwood and vermilion painted the red tikka mark on my forehead. My eyes were outlined with kohl. My lips and cheeks were rouged. The kautuka, a yellow woolen bridal thread, was fastened around my wrist. I put on my choli and my petticoat. Finally I fastened the silver earrings in my ears and wrapped the new chili-pepper-red sari as my mother instructed. I had never had so much cloth to manage. When I tucked it in properly at my waist, it was hard to walk, and it kept slipping off my head.

At last I was ready, and Baap came in to see me. I thought he would be pleased. I turned one way and the other to show off my splendor, but to my disappointment he began to cry.

"She is dressed like a woman, but she is only a child," he said.

At that I too began to cry, and it was only Maa's angry words that made us stop. After her scolding I gave her a frightened look and saw that she too had tears in her eyes.

At that moment there was a pounding on the door. "We are waiting," Mrs. Mehta called.

We heard the sound of a sitar and tabla. I looked at my parents and smiled. I must have some worth if the Mehtas were spending money for music. It did not occur to me that the music was not for me but to impress the Mehtas' friends.

A handful of people had gathered in the courtyard, where a priest was waiting. A garland of yellow and orange marigolds was placed around my neck, and I sat down across from my bride-groom. I kept my eyes down, as was proper, but I stole a quick glance at Hari. I could not hold back a small gasp of surprise, for I was sure there must have been a mistake. The boy sitting across from me seemed no older than I was, perhaps even younger. He was thin and pale and very frightened-looking. His eyes were fringed with long lashes, and he had a sulky mouth turned down at the corners.

Still, he was surely the bridegroom; I saw that his forehead had been painted, and he wore a marigold garland. Upon his head was the bride-groom's headdress, with its tassels of tinsel. The priest reached out for our hands and joined them under a small cloth of silk. Hari's hand was hot and sweaty. I nearly pulled my own hand away, but he was hanging on to it hard, as if it were keeping him from falling over.

I heard his voice for the first time as he repeated the marriage words. It was very faint, and every few minutes he had to stop to cough and clear his throat. Even in such a voice, the verses touched me:

"I am the words, thou the melody; I the seed, thou the bearer; the heaven I, the earth thou." As he said the words, the priest tied together a corner of my sari and a bit of Hari's shirt. Finally, our heads were sprinkled with water.

After the ceremony was over, and the celebration began, there was no chance to see Hari. The women were on one side of the courtyard and the men on the other. The guests seemed interested only in the food. There were potatoes with cumin, chickpeas cooked with onion and ginger, several kinds of curries, and platters of melons and mangoes. Best of all, there was my favorite sweet, coconut cakes. The men ate first, and when it was the women's turn, the coconut cakes were all gone. I thought it very unfair that a bride should not have a coconut cake on the day of her own wedding.

I saw Baap talking angrily with Mr. Mehta. Maa would not speak to Mrs. Mehta at all. The Mehtas had given no invitation to my parents to stay on, so after the feast they came to say good-bye to me. While we were alone for a minute, Maa said, "The boy is much younger than they told us, and he is sickly."

Baap quieted her. "Don't worry our daughter. There is nothing to be done now. You heard them say he is ill with flu. He will soon be over his sickness. As for his age, there is plenty of time for him to grow into a man."

Before they left, Baap brushed my hand with his and slipped me a coconut cake.

It was night when the last guest left. Mrs. Mehta, who as Hari's mother was now my sass, took my arm, holding it as I have seen women in the marketplace holding a chicken's neck before they killed it.

"You can sleep in Chandra's room," she said. "Hari is sick. He must stay with us so that I can take proper care of him. Take off your silver earrings and give them to me for safekeeping."

From what I had overheard my maa and baap say, I had guessed that the Mehtas had not been honest with us. How could I trust Mrs. Mehta now? Stubbornly I shook my head. I knew if I defied her now, we would be enemies, but I didn't care.

"What have I done to deserve so disobedient and willful a daughter-in-law?" Sass snapped at me, and left the room in a huff.

Later, when Chandra was out of the room, I hunted until I found a loose mud brick in the wall. I pried it out, hid the earrings, and replaced the brick, carefully brushing away any dirt that might give the hiding place away. In a house where there were secrets, I would have a secret of my own.

When Chandra returned, she smiled at me and took my hand in hers. "You will be my sister now," she said.

For the first time that day I felt a little happiness. Truth be told, I would rather have had a sister than a husband, especially a husband like the one I had. Chandra lay down on her charpoy, and I lay down on mine. In no time Chandra was asleep.

I slept very little that night, kept awake by my longing for my home and by Hari's coughing in the next room. As I lay there in the strange house, I felt

like a newly caged animal that rushes about looking for the open door that isn't there. I thought I
might be able to endure one day in my new home
and perhaps two, but I did not see how I could live
there for the rest of my life.

t w o

I was up early, dressing quietly while Chandra still slept. All traces of the wedding had disappeared, and the house and courtyard were bare and unfamiliar. When I looked about for even the small comforts of my own home, a worn rug or a lumpy cushion, there were none to be seen.

My sass was scooping rice from a pan into a bowl. "Stir the rice while I take this to Hari," she said.

"I could take it to . . ." I paused. Husband was too serious a word, and it would have been unseemly of me to call him by his name.

She gave me a sharp look. "I will see to Hari. Don't let the rice burn."

Mr. Mehta, my sassur, left early in the day for

the school where he taught. Chandra took the washing to the nearby river. Hari stayed in his room. I was left alone with Sass, who found one task after another for me. I took the bowls to the well in the courtyard and scoured them with ashes and sand. I returned to scour them a second time when Sass found a bit of stickiness on one of the bowls. "How were you brought up, girl?" she scolded, not even calling me by my name. I led the cow out to the field in the morning and brought her back in the afternoon for my sass to milk, but the cow was so thin, I could not see how there would be much milk. Late in the afternoon Sass went off to the village to get medicine for Hari, saying she could not trust a girl my age to get what was needed.

"You're not to bother Hari," she said as she left. "He needs his rest. I'll be gone only a short time."

When I heard Hari cough, I knew he must be awake. It did not seem fair to keep a wife from her husband. Chandra was busy in the courtyard carrying water from the well to the small vegetable garden, where squashes and melons were creeping about, looking for room to grow. There was a mango tree with fragrant flowers in the courtyard. Though Chandra warned me not to, I gathered a handful of the blossoms and took them to Hari's room.

Hari was sitting up in bed. Sprinkled all around the bed were leaves from the healing neem tree. He was looking very pale, but he seemed pleased to see me. "I brought you these," I said, laying the blossoms on his bed. As my eyes grew accustomed to the dim room, I noticed with amazement that pinned onto the mud-brick walls was an endless array of butterflies and bugs. There must have been a hundred of them, all different. I walked about looking at the butterflies' bright colors and the bugs' strange shapes. "Where did they all come from?" I asked.

Proudly he said, "They are my collection. When I was well, I gathered them. Since I have been sick, people bring them to me. I know the name of every one. If you see a bug or a butterfly, you must bring it to me."

"I could bring you bugs, though I don't like to

pick them up. But I wouldn't want to stick butter-flies to the wall."

"You have to do what I tell you because you are my wife, and besides I'm not well."

"Are you very sick?"

He was holding one of the blossoms, touching the petals. "Yes," he said. His voice was hoarse from coughing. He gave me a sulky look. "They shouldn't leave me alone with no one here to fetch me something if I need it." He peered at me from under his long eyelashes. When I did not reply, he said, "I heard the doctor say I will die."

"I don't believe you!" My heart was pounding, though, for I did believe him. Lying there in his bed without his wedding garments, he looked thin as a willow twig and very weak. I was sure he had a fever, for though the day was cool, his hair lay in damp curls on his forehead, and there was a red spot high on each cheek.

"They're going to take me to Varanasi," Hari said. "They think bathing in the Ganges will make me well. I don't think anything will make me well."

"How can you say that?" I asked. I felt myself

trembling. How could he speak so calmly about his death?

Hari went on, "If I am very lucky, I will die in Varanasi so that my ashes will be scattered over the holy Ganges River; then my spirit will be free." His whole body shook with coughing.

"I'll be right back," I said, and fled the room. Part of me wanted to escape Hari's shocking words, and part of me wanted to find a way to help him. I remembered how my maa had given me honey and ginger when I had a bad cold. I found a ginger root to grate. I had to stick my fingers in several jars before I discovered the honey. It was hidden away in the back of the cupboard.

Hari took three spoonfuls of the honey and ginger. After a few minutes, when the coughs grew fewer, he smiled at me.

"Tell me about your home," he ordered. It seemed that all his requests were commands.

I brought my quilt, climbing on Hari's bed the better to show it to him. "This is my maa and baap and my brothers and our cow, which we had to sell so I could marry you. This is our marketplace, where my baap has a stall to write letters." I showed him the spice merchants and the vegetable stalls and the man with the basket of cobras. I was so lost in amusing Hari with the pictures on my quilt, I didn't hear his maa come into the room.

"What are you doing here, girl! Get off Hari's bed! Why have you stolen the honey?" She flung the quilt at me and snatched the blossoms from the bed. "You have torn the mango flowers from the tree." While I stood there trembling, she counted the blossoms. "There are six of them. Six blossoms that will never be fruit. You have robbed us of six mangoes. I will remember that when we share out the fruit."

Hari gave his maa a sullen look. "Koly brought me the flowers to cheer me. No one else has brought flowers. She was telling me stories of her home, and she gave the honey to me for my cough. It made it better."

Hari's maa looked closely at him. "I doubt it is the honey, but I can give it to you as well as she can." She turned to me. "Leave the boy, now. He needs rest. You can make the fire for our dinner." Her voice was not so angry. She could see for herself that Hari was coughing less.

I found Hari's sister, Chandra, soaking the lentils for dinner.

"Chandra," I whispered, hardly daring to speak the terrible words aloud. "Is it true Hari is going to die?"

She answered in an even quieter whisper. "It's what the doctor warns us of. There is no medicine that can cure him." There were tears in her sad eyes. "It's why Maa and Baap are taking him to Varanasi. They hope the Ganges will make him better."

"Will you and I go to Varanasi too?" I had heard of the holy city all of my life. It would be a great thing to see. But after I asked, I was ashamed to think I wanted pleasure from so unhappy a trip.

"No. Only Maa and Baap will go. They have friends to stay with, but the railway fare is expensive."

"Chandra, I don't understand why they let Hari get married to me when he was so sick. Why did they lie to my parents about his age? Hari can't be sixteen."

Chandra looked over her shoulder to be sure we were alone. In a voice so quiet I had to lean close to her to hear, she said, "My parents needed money for the doctor and money to take Hari to Varanasi. They believe the Ganges is his last hope. A dowry was the only way they could get the money."

It was not I who was wanted at all. It was the money. I felt as if I were tangled like a small fly in the web of a cunning spider. If Hari died, what would become of me? I would be a widow whom no one would want. I had been told stories of terrible days long ago when widows were thrown on the burning funeral pyres of their husbands. I couldn't imagine that Sass would do such a thing, but the thought made me shiver.

I was very angry at the Mehtas, but after listening all day to Hari's terrible coughing, I began to think that if the Ganges could cure Hari, our wedding would not be such a bad thing.

That evening, when Hari's baap returned home, there was a terrible quarrel in Hari's room. I heard

Hari's voice and then his maa's and his baap's. Everyone was shouting. When Hari began coughing, his maa began to cry. Suddenly there was a loud crash.

I jumped. "What was that?" I asked Chandra.

"It's only Hari throwing something. He always does that when he doesn't get his way."

"Do your parents allow such behavior?"

"They never scold him. They let him have his way because he is their only son and he is so sick."

We could hear the angry voices through the thin walls. "Hari, listen to reason," his maa said. "She would only be in the way, and we cannot afford it."

"I won't go without her," Hari shouted in a hoarse voice. "She's my wife now. It's her money that is taking us."

Hari's baap tried to quiet his wife. "All this arguing is very bad for Hari. It must stop. We can take a child's pass on the railway for the girl, and she won't eat much."

"Tell her to come and see me," Hari said.

Hari's maa sounded tired. "You've had your

way. That's enough. Now you must rest."

"I want to see her." There was another crash.

A moment later Hari's maa stood beside me. "Go to your husband," she said in a cross voice.

He was sitting up in his bed, the two spots on his cheeks redder than ever. He had a sly look on his face. "I fixed it so you can come with us," he said. "You must tell me more stories about your village and the people who live there. You must obey me."

I wanted to tell him that he was only my age and in bed besides. I did not see how he could make me do something unless I wanted to. But I was grateful to him for making his parents take me to Varanasi. Besides, I was afraid that if I answered him back, Hari would start coughing or throw something.

I settled cross-legged on the floor beside his charpoy and began the story of the man who came to ask my baap to write to the government because the government's train killed his cow. As everyone knows, cows are sacred to Hindus, so it was a serious thing. The man was upset. Letters went back and forth. After many weeks the government sent a letter saying they must have proof that the cow had been killed. The man said he would send the cow's bones. The government said how could they tell whose bones the cow's were? The bones of someone else's cow might be sent. The man was so angry with the government for doubting his honesty that he wouldn't send them any more letters. Two years later a man from the government came to the village bringing a fine cow for the man, but the man said the government had insulted him, and he refused to take the cow.

Hari laughed so at the story that his coughing became worse, and his maa sent me angrily from the room.

Later in the day a doctor came. After he examined Hari, he stood in the courtyard with Hari's maa and baap. I crept close to listen. "Do as you like," the doctor said, "but if it were my son, I would not subject him to such a journey." The doctor's voice was very solemn. "I cannot hold out much hope for him. His tuberculosis is of a new kind that does not respond to medication. Still, with complete rest he may have weeks, perhaps months to live."

After the doctor left, Hari's maa asked in an impatient voice, "Are we to listen to such a man when the waters of the Ganges River are waiting?"

Hari's baap said, "The doctor is a learned man. He must know of what he speaks."

"He may be learned about his medicine, but what does he know of the healing power of the Ganges?"

As in everything, Hari's baap allowed his wife to make the decision. That night the bhagat, the local healer, came and chanted over Hari while brushing him with the leaves of a neem tree to give him strength for our trip to Varanasi the following morning.

three

In the morning there was a great rush to get ready for the trip. When the wagon came to take us to the railroad station, Hari was carried out under a little tent of cloth to protect him from the dust along the road. A woman from the village came to stay with Chandra. The two of them stood in the courtyard to see us leave. "I wish you were coming," I whispered to Chandra.

She only shook her head. Her sad eyes seemed to say it was foolishness to expect such a thing. "When you return," she said, "I have only to touch you and I will share in your darshan, your sight of the holy Ganges. That is all I ask."

I kissed Chandra and said good-bye. For a

moment I wished I might stay behind. I imagined the two of us sitting in the courtyard, chattering away under the mango tree, without Sass there to scold, and with no worries about Hari.

As I was about to leave, Chandra said, "If something happens, see that Hari has a garland of marigolds from me." She turned and fled into the house. I shuddered as I realized what she meant.

We had not even reached the railway station when I began to see that the journey was going to be very hard on Hari. The sun beat down on the tent, and the dust found its way through the floor-boards of the wagon. The road was rough, and Hari's head wobbled on his neck like a flower too large for its stem. He complained about being hot and thirsty. Twice Sass gave him water, and still he could not stop coughing.

The railway was even worse. All my pleasure in my first railway journey was lost over my worry about Hari. Along with a rush of other people, we squeezed onto the third-class coach. I felt the sharp pokes of elbows in my side and the crush of other people's feet treading on my feet. Everyone carried bundles. There were many people like Hari who were ill and going to the Ganges to be cured, but they were all older. When the passengers in the railway car saw how sick and how young Hari was, they made room for him so that at least he had a seat. The crowds and the heat made it hard to breathe. Sassur tried in vain to protect Hari from the crowds, while Sass bent over, fanning him with a palm leaf.

Just before the train pulled out, I saw several urns being loaded onto the baggage compartment of the train. I knew they contained the ashes of dead people. They were being taken to Varanasi so they could be scattered over the Ganges. I thought it inauspicious that Hari should be on a train with so many dead people. I wanted to believe that the Ganges would make Hari better, but when I looked at Hari, my hope slipped away like a frightened mouse into a dark hole.

The journey took four hours. We had brought cooked rice and a melon to slice. Sass urged Hari to have some, but he would not eat. Much of the time he slept, which was a mercy, for he coughed less in his sleep. Once, when I looked at Sass, I saw that tears were running down her cheeks.

From the train window I watched as miles of flat land went speeding by. As we neared a village, the train slowed, came to a stop, and gave us all a good shake. The jerk of the train woke Hari, who looked about in a dazed way and then drifted off to sleep again. At every stop new crowds pushed into the car to squeeze into what little space remained. Once, when I looked out the window, I saw washerwomen stretching out lengths of saris to dry in the sun, long strips of yellow and blue and pink against the green fields. At one stop I heard the name of a village called. I knew the place well; it was walking distance from my own village. It was all I could do to keep from jumping from the train and running down the dusty, familiar road to my home and my maa and baap and my brothers. They would have no idea I was so close. As much as I longed to see them, though, I knew that after all the sacrifices they had made for my dowry, I would shame them by returning home.

We reached Varanasi late in the afternoon. The city in all its confusion seemed too large for us. It was several minutes before we knew which way to turn. We pushed past crowds of beggars. Sassur paused to drop coins into their cups, for the giving of alms brings one much credit with the gods. He clutched the address of his old friend Mr. Lal, a Brahman scholar, who had invited us to stay with him. Sassur found two bicycle rickshaws. After bargaining with the rickshaw wallahs, Sass settled Hari and Sassur in one rickshaw and directed me to join her in the second one.

The streets were crowded with motorcycles, automobiles, bicycles, and horse-drawn tongas. People clung to buses like swarms of bees on a branch. Cows and dogs and goats wandered in and out of the traffic. I even saw a camel.

Hari's face was flushed, and like me he was looking about in amazement. "Look there!" he whispered hoarsely. In this city of fifteen thousand shrines, each shrine was more splendid than the next, but he was pointing to the great mosque of Aurangzeb, where the city's Muslims worshiped. Its eight towers were like lanterns suspended from the sky.

Just before we turned off onto a narrow street, we caught a glimpse of the Golden Temple of Vishvanath and the great river itself, Maa Ganges. "How soon will we go?" Hari asked in a weak voice.

"When you are rested, Hari," Sassur said.

Hari closed his eyes and made no reply. His silence broke my heart. All of Hari's sullenness and temper were gone, and without them Hari seemed to be disappearing.

Mr. Lal and his wife greeted us warmly. They were elderly and very stately. I was not introduced as Hari's wife. I believe they took me for his sister. I wondered if Hari's parents were ashamed to admit before this dignified man that they had married so young and so sick a son to get money. Mrs. Lal brought us a meal of dal and chapatis. Mr. Lal brought a small jar of water. With great ceremony he held it out to Hari. In a solemn voice he said, "From the Ganges."

We all watched, holding our breath and hoping

for some miracle, while Hari drank the water. But there was no miracle that we could see, only Hari suffering a new attack of coughing.

Though everyone was eager to take Hari to the river, he was too weakened from the long journey to go. Just before we lay down to sleep, Mrs. Lal gave Sass some mustard oil and camphor to rub on Hari's chest. The next morning he seemed a little better.

After a quick meal of tea and lentils we set off. Two men were hired to carry Hari's cot. With Mr. Lal and Sass and Sassur, we began our pilgrimage to the Golden Temple. We could hardly move, for like us, half the city was making its way to the river. There were women wearing saris the color of jewels, many of them woven with gold. There were holy men whose faces were covered with ashes and who wore nothing at all. There were Jains with masks tied around their faces so they wouldn't acci-dentally breathe in an insect and so kill a living thing, which was against their religion. There were Sikhs from the Punjab who never cut their hair but tucked it all up under their turbans. In their saffron robes, sadhus, holy men, were everywhere. They carried begging bowls, and the air was heavy with their chants.

When I looked into the temples, I could see the holy sadhus sitting in long rows, bare chested, their heads shaven, holding sacred lamps and accompanying their chanting with bells. Pigeons fluttered in and out of the temple's open doorways. I looked at Hari to see if he was as astonished as I at such sights. When I caught his eye, a faint smile came over his face. I thought he might have been telling me that I had him to thank for so wondrous a trip.

At last we came to the Golden Temple of Vishvanath. A ghat, a long, wide flight of steps, led down to the river. With the two men holding Hari's cot between them, we made our way down the ghat, pushing through the crowds. Hari had to hang on to the cot to keep from slipping off.

Along the river's edge women were scrubbing clothes and even washing their pots and pans. Barbers were cutting hair. There were dogs and a cow wandering about. Two boys were flying kites. We saw people with every kind of illness. Some could not walk; others were as thin and wasted as Hari was; some had terrible sores and deformities. I could hardly bear to look at all the misery. Yet the expressions on the faces of the sick were not sad. They were not hopeful, but they were peaceful. Even Hari looked more comfortable and content.

The crowds on either side of us and behind us swept us forward. Ahead of us was Maa Ganges. As the pilgrims reached the greenish-brown river, they walked right into the water. They faced the morning sun and began their pujas, reciting their prayers and making their offerings of flowers or grain. The saris of the wading women floated on the surface of the water like the petals of pond lilies. Beyond the pilgrims hundreds of small boats skimmed over the river.

Sassur and Mr. Lal helped Hari from his cot and eased him into the water. As the water slid over his body, Hari appeared surprised, as if he could not believe that at long last Maa Ganges was wrapping herself about him.

I did not know whether I might be allowed to step into the water myself. When I looked at Sass, she nodded her head. It was still early in the morning, and the water felt cool on my legs. I waited, not knowing what to expect. Hari had been too weak to walk to the river on his own legs, but now the river seemed to strengthen him. He had taken his shirt off to bathe, and I could see draped over his left shoulder the sacred thread given to Brahman boys when they come of age. He called out to me, "Koly, look here. I can make myself float. Try it for yourself." Hari played about in the water, even splashing me. For the first time I could see what Hari must have been like before he became so sick. I thought he was very like my brothers.

Sassur was shocked. "This is not a game, son. It is a sacred river to be treated with respect." Though he scolded, I saw that he was pleased at Hari's liveliness.

Hari's liveliness did not last. He had to be helped from the river. He was shivering and then feverish. When we returned to Mr. Lal's house, Hari was put to bed at once. His coughing became so bad that a Varanasi doctor was called. The doctor wore a proper black suit and carried a black bag. When at last he came out of Hari's room, he looked very solemn. Speaking in a low voice so Hari could not hear, the doctor said, "I am sorry to have to tell you this, but the boy is gravely ill. There is nothing to be done."

It took me a moment to understand what the doctor meant. I turned to Sass, and we held on to each other. We were both crying. If she wished me gone, or I believed her unkind, neither of us thought of such things now. All that was in our minds was our worry over Hari. I had not known Hari for very long, but I remembered the verses said at our wedding by the priest: "I am the words, thou the melody; I the seed, thou the bearer; the heaven I, the earth thou." How could all that be with just one of us? I couldn't understand what was happening to Hari and me.

After the doctor left, Mr. Lal said in his quiet

voice, "At least your son will die in Varanasi." Though he meant his words kindly, they did little to comfort us.

No one slept that night. Hari's coughing grew louder. I heard the voices and footsteps of people hurrying back and forth. In the middle of the night the doctor came again. After he went into Hari's room, there was silence. A moment later I heard a terrible wailing. I knew it was Sass and that there could be only one reason for such a cry. I folded myself into as small a ball as I could and pulled the quilt over my head to drown out the frightening sound.

When Sassur came in to tell me of Hari's death, I would not listen. He sat down beside me and put a hand on my shoulder. "We should never have let you marry our son," he said. "It was not fair to you. We only wanted him to get well. We thought if we could bring him to the holy river, there would be a chance. You must be like a daughter to us now." At last I heard his heavy steps going away.

Whatever my sassur had said, I knew Sass

would never think of me as a daughter. I was nothing now. I could not go back to my parents and be a daughter again. I was no longer a wife or a bahus, a daughter-in-law. Yes, I thought, I am something. I am a widow. And I began to sob.

In the morning Hari's body was wrapped in a cloth and covered with garlands of marigolds. I put one of the garlands on him for Chandra. Hari was carried on a bamboo platform through the streets to the Ganges. Walking behind the platform were Mr. Lal and his wife, Hari's parents and I, and a priest who was a friend of Mr. Lal's. As we walked along, we chanted over and over, "Rama nama satya hai," "The name of Rama is truth."

This time the crowds did not push past us but stood a little aside to let us by. A few men joined in our chants and followed us for a short distance. There were many processions like ours that morning, all moving toward the Ganges. Some of the processions were accompanied by music and dancing, for in the midst of the sorrow there was happiness that the death had taken place in Varanasi.

Only the men accompanied Hari's body to the Manikarnika Ghat for the cremation. After the cremation the scattering of Hari's ashes over the Ganges would set his soul free by returning his body to fire, water, and earth. As we three women waited at a respectable distance, we clung to one another. I could hear the men recite the chants for the dead; Hari's voice was to go to the sky, his eyes to the sun, his ear to the heavens, his body to the earth, and his thoughts to the moon. Finally we heard the words "Amar rahain," "Live eternally," and the ceremony was over.

When the men returned, we made our way quietly back toward the Lals' house. As we walked through the Golden Temple, a dove wove a pattern just above our heads. I knew that the spirit of the dead hovers about for a time, and the swooping dove seemed very like Hari.

Before we left Varanasi, Sass purchased a cheap white cotton sari for me. "It is what widows wear," she said.

four

When I returned home with Hari's parents, everything was different. We all tiptoed by the room where Hari had slept as if any noise would awaken him. I felt his not being there more than I had felt his being there. There was little talk in the house. We all moved silently about our tasks. As the days passed, Sass had little to say to me, addressing me only to give an order or to scold me for not carrying the order out as she wished.

I was glad to have Chandra with me. When Chandra mourned for her brother, we put our arms around each other. When I woke in the middle of the night to find the room full of ghosts, the reassuring sound of her soft breathing sent them away. She told me what Hari was like when he was growing up. I told her of my own brothers. Chandra had movie magazines that we looked at together. One night a fruit bat flew through our window, and we hid, giggling, under the covers until it was gone.

A few weeks after Hari's death Sass told me to put on my widow's white sari. "We are going into the village," she said, but she would not tell me why. She hurried us past the outskirts of the village, where the untouchables had homes made of bits of metal and old crates. "You must not let their shadow fall upon you," she warned, "or it will pollute you."

Sass seemed to take pleasure in finding someone who was worse off than she was, while I could not believe there was anyone more miserable than I was.

Sass led me to the government office, where there was an official wearing a suit, shirt, tie, and jacket. As we approached the official, Sass warned me in a low whisper, "There will be no need for you to talk. I will explain."

"What is there to explain?" I whispered. Sass only gave my arm a yank and propelled me into the office.

"Sir," Sass said to the man, "my son has died. This is his widow. Does the government not have something for her?"

The man gave me a quick glance, and after saying he was very sorry to hear of Hari's death, he pushed some papers at Sass and me to sign. Since neither of us could read the papers, Sass said she would take them home so that her husband, who was a scholar, could read them. Then she would return them with our marks.

When we were outside the office, I asked, "What does the government have for me?"

Sass brushed aside my question. "It is a way of speaking. The papers are only to record Hari's death." I was sure there was more to it, but the mention of Hari's death had set her to weeping, and I could do nothing but trail along behind her as she hurried home with her misery.

After that, each month an envelope with a government stamp came for me. "It is official business," Sass would say, taking it from the postman, "and nothing for you to bother about."

In her sadness over Hari's death Sass grew
bitter. Her angry words buzzed around me, stinging
like wasps. "Your dowry did not save Hari, and
now we are burdened with one more mouth to
feed," she scolded. She made my own name hateful
to me. All day long she sent it screaming through
the house and across the courtyard: *"Koly, we need
water!" "Koly, sweep the courtyard! The geese have
soiled it." "Koly, the clothes you washed are still
dirty!" "Koly, the spices you ground for the masalas
are too coarse!"*

I did the best I could, thankful for a bed to sleep
on and food to put in my mouth. Each morning I
got up before the sun swallowed the darkness. It
was so early that I felt as if I were the only one
awake in the world. I made a respectful puja, bow-
ing to the household shrine. I washed at the courtyard well and brushed my teeth with a twig from
the neem tree. I gathered dried leaves to light the
dung in the stove so the water for tea would be
boiling when the family awoke. I slapped the cow
dung into nicely shaped cakes and plastered them

to the walls, a neat handprint on each one. After the sun dried them, they would feed the fire. I hurried to the well for a pail of water. When you hold water in your hand, it weighs nothing, but put it in a pail and it is as heavy as a stone! I threw sticks at the bandicoot, the nasty rat that lived under the house, to keep it from getting our food.

If Sass had let me creep quietly about my tasks, I would have been content. I still would have had a little place inside me to go, a place I could wrap myself in like the cocoon a caterpillar makes. You can touch the cocoon, but you cannot touch the little thing inside unless you tear it apart. That is what my sass was doing to me, worrying and badgering me with her never-ending orders and scoldings.

She screamed at me, "You are no better than the bandicoot that burrows under our house and eats our food. Go home to your miserable parents!" But she knew as well as I that I could not go back to my village. It would have been a terrible disgrace to return like a hungry dog to my parents' home.

To comfort myself, I began a quilt. When I

explained to Sass that the quilt would be a way to remember Hari, for once she was not angry with me but only cautioned me to finish my tasks before taking up the quilt. She gave me rags for the quilt and a few rupees to buy thread. Though she pretended to take no notice of my work, even complaining that I was neglecting my tasks, I would sometimes come upon her looking to see what I had stitched. I embroidered Hari in his bridegroom's headdress as the two of us sat before the priest. I stitched the train that took us to Varanasi, and Hari splashing about in the river. At last I made the procession to the Ganges with Hari's body covered with garlands. All around the edge of the quilt I put a border of bugs and butterflies.

In February on the night of the full moon we could hear the sound of drums in the distance. It was Holi, the feast that celebrates the god Krishna's love for the fair Radha. At first Sass would not allow Chandra and me to go into the village. At Holi a special red powder mixed with cow's dung and urine is thrown at everyone. But Chandra kept pleading, and finally, after we promised to wear our oldest clothes, we were allowed to go. To our surprise Sass decided to go with us. She said it was to see that we behaved, but I believe she was glad of an excuse to leave the sadness of the house.

In no time everyone was covered with the red dye. Small boys ran about squirting everyone with their water guns. Late in the evening, when the dancing became wild, Sass hurried us home. But for a few hours we had forgotten our troubles.

When the hot weather came, I worked on the quilt in the courtyard, hoping for a little breeze. Day after day the heat pressed down on us. I longed to be like the turtles in the dried-out streams, hidden in the mud, waiting for the rains to give them life again.

Chandra loved to watch me embroider. "Your needle makes the pictures come alive," she said.

"I can teach you," I offered, but Chandra only shook her head.

"I'd rather watch you," she said.

Chandra was not lazy, but only a little spoiled. She was allowed to sleep later than I was in the morning, was given more food to eat, and had fewer tasks than I did, always the easier ones like airing the quilts and pillows. Still, I could not be angry with her for the way Sass treated me. Chandra was willing enough to help me, but she gave little thought to a task. She was always dreaming of something else—the shape of the clouds or the color of the sari she had seen in the marketplace or, most often, the husband she would have one day.

I sometimes teased her for her daydreams, but I was happy to have her for a sister. If Sass scolded me, Chandra would find an excuse for me. When she was given some treat to eat that was not given to me, she would secretly save some and give it to me when we were alone. Chandra had tied a rope to the mango tree, knotting the end. When Sass was busy elsewhere, we hung on to the rope and swung ourselves into the treetops.

The best parts of the days were the afternoons, when Chandra and I had the courtyard to ourselves for our baths. We took turns pouring pails of water over each other. We would unwind our saris. Only then, as the cool water washed over me, could I forget Sass's scalding words and the fiery sun. We would put on fresh, dry clothes, making sure all the while that no parts of our bodies showed, so as to preserve our modesty.

I sometimes looked into Hari's room. The bugs had dried up and fallen to the floor. The butterflies had lost their color. His room was now used to store flour and lentils. A stray cat often slept there. It would gaze at me with its sly brown eyes just as Hari had done. One of Hari's schoolbooks still lay on the trunk. No one touched the book, and day by day the dust grew on it. Though I could not read, I sometimes opened the book and looked at the words. They were words that Hari had known.

I thought it would be a fine thing to have a book of my own. No one seemed to want it, and I began to think of asking for it, wondering if such a request would be met with a new round of scoldings. One evening I gathered my courage and went to Sassur. I blurted out, "May I have Hari's schoolbook?"

Sassur always seemed surprised to find I was

still there. After staring at me for a moment, he said, "It would fetch only a rupee or two in the marketplace. Take it. But what will you do with it? Can you read?"

I shook my head. "I thought if I turned the pages over and over, I might learn."

I expected Sassur to laugh at my foolishness. Instead he gave me a long look. For the first time since Hari's death I saw his smile. "Say nothing to your sass, but come to me each evening when she is talking in the courtyard with the neighbor women. I'll help you to learn to read and write."

That night I could not keep the happy news to myself. "Chandra," I whispered, "your baap is going to teach me to read. You can learn as well."

Chandra shook her head. "I could never learn such things."

"Yes, you could."

"I have no need. My parents are looking for a husband for me."

After that I went each evening to my sassur. He showed me how each word is a little package of letters. He was clever with a pencil. For each letter he drew a picture of some creature, a hawk or a pig, and printed its name below the letter. When I had all the letters, he drew a railway. The engine pulled several words, so that now I had a sentence. Page by page I learned the secrets in the book. What was even more exciting, Sassur told me there were many books, each one with a story in it. As the months went on, he gave me some of those other books to read. Chandra and I were not allowed oil to light our room at night. In order to read the books, I had to take them with me, hidden in my sari, when I went to wash the clothes in the river. I hurried to finish the washing so I would have a little time with my book.

I looked forward to those walks to the river, for I was walking away from Sass and her scolding. It was June and hot summer now. The dry bamboo leaves rattled in the wind. Puffs of dust exploded with my every step. Along the road I saw women winnowing baskets of threshed grain in the wind, the clouds of chaff flying off in the breeze. The mustard fields were golden with blossoms and smelled fragrant when I walked by them. In this dry season only a trickle of muddy water remained in the river. Though I rubbed the clothes on the stones to get them clean, the clothes sometimes looked even dirtier when I was finished.

Still, I loved the river. Sometimes a tiny silver fish would leap from the water after a fly. Hawks circled overhead. Bright-green dragonflies wove in and out of the reeds. A kingfisher perched on a peepul tree, its red breast like a tongue of fire. I washed the dust off my bare feet and splashed the water over me for the coolness. I thought of how Hari had splashed me in the Ganges. I wondered what my life would have been like as Hari's wife. I knew that Hari had been spoiled and would not have been easy to live with, yet I was sure I would have been happier than I was now.

There were days at the river when I did not pick up my book but only daydreamed like Chandra. I imagined myself returning to my village, to my maa and baap and my brothers. I wanted to picture welcoming looks on their faces when they saw me come back to them in my widow's sari. As hard as I tried, I could not put such looks on their faces, nor could I feel their welcoming embraces. Instead I saw them all lined up in the courtyard, frowning and cross. I heard them order me back to the home of my husband's parents. "It is where you belong now," they would surely say.

Sometimes I would picture myself running away, selling my earrings to get a railway ticket to Varanasi. I thought of the excitement of the city. But what would I do for a living, and where could I stay? I remembered all the families living on the streets. Though I turned these things over and over in my head, I did not see how I could escape.

As the summer days grew hotter and hotter, Chandra and I would stand in the courtyard every afternoon, looking up at the sky, waiting for the rains to cool us. One day just as we had given up hope, huge gray clouds, large and clumsy as elephants, came rolling in. A moment later a million pails of water emptied on us. Holding hands, we danced and danced, tipping our heads up and opening our mouths. Our clothes clung to us, and under our feet the dry dust of the courtyard softened into mud and squeezed up between our toes.

Even Sass forgot her scolding and stood a little apart in the courtyard letting the rain fall on her as if it were washing away some of her sorrow.

Now that the monsoon had come, everything was damp. The quilts on our beds and the clothes in our chest were limp and smelled of mildew. Overnight our sandals turned green with mold. In every room water dripped down from the ceiling, so when we had a hard rain outside, it was like a small rain shower inside. The mud-brick walls of the house became even thinner. A part of the roof caved in.

Overnight the wilting wheat and millet fields turned green. Mosquitoes bred in the little pools along the roadside. We could not walk very far without snakes for company. They were everywhere, hanging from the mango tree and crawling under our charpoys so that we were afraid to sleep. Sassur had to come to our room with a big branch and beat the invading snakes to death.

Though we were refreshed by the rain, there were still scoldings from Sass. Either I did not rub the clothes hard enough to get them clean or I rubbed them so hard they were worn thin. One day she accused me of putting too much water in the rice, so that it was like gruel. The next day she said I did not put in enough water, and the rice was dry as dust. If I answered back, I was impudent. If I kept silent, I was sullen. I saw that no matter how hard I worked, I could never please her.

At the end of summer Krishna's birthday was celebrated. It was a national holiday, and Sassur took Chandra and me into the village to see the fireworks. The colors exploded like handfuls of petals tossed into the sky. There were trained monkeys and clever starlings that had been taught to talk. There was a man who rode a bicycle on a tightrope and a snake charmer whose cobra was so old and lazy, it could not be coaxed from its basket and had to be tumbled out. Sassur gave us a few coins to buy a cone of spun sugar. We each ate half and laughed at how our faces were sticky all over with pink sugar.

Though Sassur was kind to me and had taught me to read, I could not turn to him for help. He left early in the morning for school and came home with papers to correct. He was paid very little for his teaching and often appeared troubled.

"Is the teaching very hard?" I once asked him.

"The teaching would be nothing, but my students are rude and disrespectful. They hide my glasses so that I cannot see the lesson. Last week they put a scorpion on my desk."

"How can that be? They should be grateful to you."

He smiled at me. "Ah, Koly, I only wish my students were as anxious to learn as you are."

Sassur suffered from more than the students' tricks. When he was home, Sass was always complaining about how poor they were and how others were better off. I think Sassur was as miserable as I was.

The only time my sassur seemed to come alive was when he had a book in his hand. Now that I could read, he often took out a book of poems by the great Indian poet Rabindranath Tagore. The book had a fine leather cover with its title in gold letters. The inside covers had fancy colored paper on them. The most impressive thing was Tagore's own signature in the book.

"He signed the book for my baap," Sassur said. "My baap went to hear him give a reading of his poems. The book has been handed down from son to son, but now . . ." He sighed, and I knew he was thinking of Hari, so I began to read aloud to Sassur from my favorite poem. It was about a flock of birds flying day and night through the skies. Among them was one homeless bird, always flying on to somewhere else.

One day Sass caught us at our reading. She was very angry.

"What are you teaching that girl?" she cried. "It is no wonder she forgets to do her work."

Sass was suspicious of books, treating them as if they were scorpions and might sting her. From then on if she caught me reading, she would call me lazy and set me to a task or send me off to the village on an errand. But no matter what Sass thought, the secrets in the books were now mine, and try as she might, she could not snatch them away.

I still bowed to the household shrine each morning, but now I begged Krishna to find a way to let me escape. In my books I had read that as a child, Krishna was very mischievous. Now I became mischievous as well. The milk I churned would not turn into butter. The grain I ground for chapatis had bits of chaff that got between our teeth. In the garden I pulled up the potato plants and left the weeds. The dung cakes I made fell apart, so the fire went out. I put a dead frog in the water bottle. The bottle was brass, so no one noticed the frog until all the water had been drunk. I left the geese's mess where Sass would step into it. I looked away when the bandicoot ate the mangoes.

In one thing I was careful. I never spilled the salt, for my maa had told me in the next world you had to sweep up every grain of salt you spilled, and I didn't want to waste my time doing that.

"Why do you anger my maa?" Chandra asked. "She is like those little red ants that swarm all over you and bite and bite."

I knew what Chandra said was true, but I also knew that I could not crawl about like a beaten dog. I had heard about families that had murdered the widows of their sons to get rid of them. Though I knew Sass would never do such a thing, I believed she would surely kill my spirit with her spitefulness if I didn't fight back.

I would not let Sass's scoldings touch me as they used to. She became smaller in my mind. I had the comfort of Chandra, for we were as sisters now, and each evening after my work was finished, my books were there to welcome me. In this way two years passed, and then whispering began in the house. Sass and Sassur spoke in low voices. Chandra began to wear a secret smile. One night she confided to me, "The gataka has found me a husband."

five

Soon Sass and Sassur consulted an astrologer, and Chandra was dancing with excitement. "The astrologer brought out his charts, and after much study he named January second as the most auspicious day." She told me with great importance, "The gataka has done well for me. The bridegroom, Raman, is nineteen and has been to mission school. Already he has written to an uncle who has promised him a job working with computers."

"Computers!" I had heard of such a thing from my own baap. "One day they will have no need for scribes like myself," he had complained. "They will put a machine in the marketplace instead. The machine will write the letters well enough, but the words the machine writes will have no elegance and no heart."

I told Chandra, "Your bridegroom must be very learned." Though I was impressed, something was bothering me. "Chandra, how can you tell if you will love him?" I asked. "You have never seen him." Though he was dead and I knew I should not think badly of him, I remembered how disappointed I had been in Hari.

"I will learn to love him," Chandra said. "I had never seen you before you came to our house, and I learned to love you."

"What if he isn't good to you?"

"If I am a good wife, he will be good to me."

I hoped Chandra was right, but I could not help remembering a stall in the bazaar where Chandra and I had sorted through a heap of mismatched earrings. We had looked through them hoping to find two that matched. What if it was as difficult to find two matching people?

I wanted to be happy for Chandra, but I felt a sadness deep inside me. The wedding brought back all the memories of my own short marriage—all my excitement and pleasure and my hopes coming to nothing. Also, I knew how much I would miss Chandra. Now, when Sass scolded me all day long, I could bear it, for I knew I could whisper my complaints into Chandra's ear in the evening. Soon there would be no one to comfort me.

As Chandra's wedding approached, Sass came to me one day. "We have no money for a new sari for Chandra," she said. "She must have your wedding sari. You need nothing but your widow's sari."

I longed to say that I did not want to spend the rest of my life dressed as a widow, but I knew Sass would be scandalized by such words. So I watched Chandra try on my sari and said nothing. With her womanly figure, her smiles, and her bright eyes, she looked very lovely.

"Chandra must have your silver earrings as well," Sass said.

Stubbornly I shook my head. I would not give up the earrings. As long as I had them, I could keep my dream of running away. I knew that if I simply refused, Sass would find a way to make me give them up. So I lied. "I have lost them," I said.

"I don't believe you!" Sass screamed. "You are an evil girl! All these days we have put a roof over your head and fed you. This is how you repay us, with selfishness."

I should have kept quiet, but I could not. "I have worked for my food," I said, "harder than anyone."

Sass squinted her eyes as she always did when she was very, very angry. In a harsh voice she said, "You do not know the meaning of work. You idle about with your daydreams and your foolish books and your stitching. I will see to it that from now on you do indeed earn your keep."

That evening, when I should have been asleep, I crept out to the courtyard. I did not want to spoil Chandra's happiness with my misery. As I sat thinking of whether I ought to give in and hand over the earrings, I heard Sass complain of me to Sassur. "She is a wicked girl not to give Chandra her earrings. I am sure she still has them. I have searched their room but I can't find them. It was an inauspicious day when that girl came into our house."

"She is not a bad girl," Sassur said in a weary voice. "Think of what her life is like with Hari gone. She has nothing to look forward to. Remember that without her dowry we would never have had the money to go to Varanasi, and her widow's pension these two years has added to Chandra's dowry."

His last words were like a slap. Widow's pension? I didn't wait to hear more but hurried in to Chandra, who was already asleep. I shook her awake. "Chandra, is it true? Did they take my widow's pension for your dowry?"

Chandra sat up in bed and gave me a surprised look. "Didn't you know?" She looked frightened. "You wouldn't take the pension back, would you? If you do, I'll have no husband."

I was very angry, but not so angry that I would ruin Chandra's happiness. I shook my head. I did not blame Chandra for taking what was rightfully mine, but I knew I would not have done the same to her. I was more determined than ever to keep the silver earrings. They would buy me a railway ticket. The pension might go with me to keep me from starving.

It took me all night to work up my courage, but in the morning I went to Sass. Clenching my hands behind me, I took a deep breath and said in a weaker voice than I would have wished, "The next time the envelope comes from the government, it is to be handed over to me."

For just a moment Sass looked frightened, but then she quickly said, "If you are speaking of the few rupees you are sent each month, do not think they are due you. They hardly pay for your keep." She gave me a triumphant look. "If it were not for our son, you would not be a widow. So there would be no rupees at all for you." She marched out of the room.

Defeated, I stood looking after her. She was like a great boulder shutting me into a cave. I could not move her, and I could not get around her.

Despite my anger at Sass I longed to give

Chandra something for her wedding. "I wish I had money to buy you a gift," I told her.

Chandra thought for a moment. "Would you make me a quilt?" she asked. "I could take it with me, and if I became homesick, I could bring it out to remind me of you. Put in all the things we have done together."

"Your maa is angry with me over the earrings and would never give me cloth for the quilt or money to buy thread."

I was wrong. When Chandra went to her, Sass said, "It would not be such a bad thing if your dowry were to include a quilt. Let her make one if it doesn't keep her from her tasks."

I stitched a picture of our little room, the two of us sitting cross-legged on our charpoys with large smiles on our faces. There we were dancing in the rain. There was the river where we went to wash the clothes and the kingfisher that watched us from a tree. There we were sitting together in front of the village television set. I stitched the colors of the fireworks exploding into the sky on Lord Krishna's birthday and the two of us covered with red powder at the celebration of Holi. I embroidered us having our baths at the well. I put in Sass chatting with her friends in the courtyard and Sassur reading from Tagore's book of poems. I even put in the cow and the bandicoot. In a moment of mischief I made the border of blossoms from the mango tree. Sass could not scold me for stealing those blossoms, for they were all mine.

I had to squeeze in the time for the quilt, for there was much to do to prepare for the wedding. The courtyard where the wedding was to take place had to be carefully swept and a ceremonial fire readied. The walls had to be ornamented with a mixture of rice flour and water, which I dribbled through my fingers. I went to the village to buy firewood and food for the wedding feast. I peeled mangoes and chopped cucumbers and onions and mixed the turmeric and coriander for the curry.

I had to do the stitching of the quilt early in the morning or in the evening when the light was poor, so I went about with a frown from squinting.

When at last the quilt was completed, Chandra exclaimed, "Koly, it's beautiful!" and hugged it to her. Though she tried, even Sass could find no fault with it.

I had looked forward to helping prepare Chandra on her wedding day, but Sass sent me away. "It is not proper," she said. "Only those women who are not widowed and have borne a male child are privileged to help."

I knew this was the custom; still, I had hoped I might at least be allowed in the room to enjoy the ceremonies. I had to be content with a peek at Chandra when the women were finished with her. Seeing her in my wedding sari, her eyes darkened with kohl, her cheeks and lips rouged, and designs painted on her forehead, was like seeing myself again as I had been almost three years before. For Chandra's sake I smiled and told her how beautiful she looked, as indeed she did. Inside I was miserable and did not know how I would ever be happy again. My life seemed to be over. What was there to look forward to but years and years of slaving away?

When the day for the wedding came, Chandra and I hid by the window so that we could get a glimpse of the bridegroom. Led by his male relatives, Raman arrived on a horse covered with a cloth embroidered with small, round mirrors. The mirrors glittered as he rode along, so he looked like he was arriving on a shaft of sunlight. He was tall, with a great deal of wavy black hair and a small mustache.

"The mustache is like a mouse's tail," I said, giggling.

"It is not!" Chandra said. "It's a fine mustache."

We stretched our heads out the window to get a better view. Just then the bridegroom looked our way. I saw a slight smile hurry across his face as he saw us, and I began to believe Chandra's marriage might be a good one.

Sassur greeted the bridegroom with the required perfumed water and mixture of honey and curds. The guests arrived: all the relatives who lived within a day's drive, Sassur's fellow teachers, the women who gossiped with Sass in the courtyard and their husbands and children, the relatives and friends of the bridegroom who came to see how well or how poorly the parents of the bridegroom had done in their choice.

How different this wedding was from mine. Instead of a frightened gawky girl and a young and doomed bridegroom, there were a handsome young man and a happy and beautiful bride. The ceremony was soon over, and the feasting began. A tali was brought out piled with boiled ducks' eggs, crisply fried pooris, dal, rice, curries, chapatis, mango chutney, and many kinds of sweets. The food was served first to the men and then to the women guests, and last I ate with the women who had been hired to help with the cooking and serving. I did not mind being last, for I had prepared much of the food and sampled it whenever Sass's back was turned.

At last it was time for Chandra to go to the home of her bridegroom. She embraced her maa and baap. She threw her arms around me. "Koly," she whispered, "I will miss you most of all." With her face pressed against mine, I could not tell whether the tears I felt on my cheeks were hers or mine.

As I watched Chandra and her bridegroom leave for his home, I felt my last bit of happiness disappearing.

Sass was as sorry as I was to see Chandra go. She wept, moaning, "I have lost my daughter forever." Sassur disappeared into his room and took down the book of Tagore's poems, but each time I looked into the room, I saw that no page had been turned. I had no one to talk with now but the little green lizards that crept up my wall.

My pension was lost to me, and I did not know how far my earrings might take me. It seemed that I must stay where I was forever. I hoped that if I worked very hard, and did exactly as I was told, Sass might begin to look kindly upon me. I hoped that someday she might love me as she loved Chandra, or if not so much as that, at least a little.

I was sorry for the times in the past when I had been mischievous. I began to rise earlier in the morning, so early the stars were still in the sky and the snakes at the edge of the courtyard were still twined into sleepy coils waiting for the sun to warm them. Each morning I made my puja at the kitchen shrine, careful to present an offering of fruit or a few scattered flower petals. I plastered the chula, the small stove on which we cooked, with fresh mud. I set the fire, waiting until everyone was up to light it so that no fuel would be wasted. I soaked the rice before boiling it and stirred it so that it was fluffy and the grains did not stick together. I ground the spices to a fine powder with the stone roller and churned the milk carefully. I swept the courtyard morning and afternoon.

When I saw Sass sitting by herself, a sad look on her face, I said, "Let me comb your hair and braid it for you." It was something that Chandra used to do for her maa.

"No. You are too clumsy. If you have time on your hands, there are pots to scrub."

It was that way with everything I asked to do for

her. It was no better with Sassur. He had troubles of his own. The school where he taught now had electricity. Computers had been installed, and more and more responsibility was taken away from Sassur, who knew nothing about such things. When he came home in the evenings, he went to his room and closed the door. We could hear him chanting his prayers hour after hour. He would not come out for meals but took only a handful of cold rice and a chapati or two. He grew thinner, his cheeks more hollow, his neck scrawnier.

I saw that there was a bowl of rice ready for Sassur when his chanting was finished. I even offered to read some of Tagore's poems to him, but he merely shook his head. "My son is dead, my daughter is far away, and I am laughed at by my students. What is left for me? One day I will walk off across the fields, and you will see no more of me."

If Sass tried to tell him of problems in the house, he would silently climb up onto the roof of the house, pull the ladder up after himself, and resume his chants.

When I found I could no longer talk to Sassur,

I looked about for something to care for. If no one would love me, I could at least love something. A pariah dog would slink into the courtyard from time to time in search of a morsel of food. Now I began to save a bit of our dinner for the dog. Its dirty yellow fur was mangy. Its eyes were red and watery. There were sores on its back, and one foot was lame. Still, it was clever enough never to appear when Sass was about. Soon it was following me to the river where I washed the clothes. I would bathe its sores and pet it until it lost its wary look. When it curled up next to me, I could feel its warmth. Instead of slinking about and hiding in corners, it began to appear openly in the courtyard.

One afternoon Sass caught me giving the dog a bit of chapati smeared with dal. "What are you doing, girl?" she scolded. "We hardly have enough for ourselves, and you throw our food to the dogs. What can you be thinking of?" She started to chase the dog away.

At that moment a gosling waddled close to the dog, who had been cringing in a corner of the courtyard. The dog closed its teeth over the unfortunate gosling's neck. Sass ran after the dog with a stick, landing several blows. Still the dog would not let go. As it disappeared around a bend, we could still hear the squawking of the gosling. After that the dog knew better than to return.

So I tamed the bandicoot. It was an ugly animal with a pointed snout, tiny eyes, and large pointed ears. From its head to its long ratty tail it was nearly two feet long. Unlike the foolish dog, it never showed itself in the courtyard when others were there, but would come only to me. It crawled out from under the veranda on its belly and crept carefully up to me to take the bit of food I had saved from my meal. It sat hunched next to me, munching slowly as if it wanted to make the morsel last. When the food was gone, it would lick its whiskers and crawl back under the veranda. I was glad enough for the bandicoot's company, but I did not think I wanted to spend my life sweeping goose droppings from the courtyard and talking to a rat.

It was on the way to the village where Sass sent

me to buy some chilis and a paper of cumin that the idea came to me. I ran the rest of the way to the village so that I should have a few extra minutes there. When I reached the village, I made my way to the office where we had been given the papers that brought my pension. Through the open door I could see the man who had given us the papers to sign, but his very dark suit and very white shirt frightened me away. Twice more when I was in the village, I went to look into the office, and twice more I hurried away, too timid to speak to a man dressed so formally. Then one evening I saw the same man walking past our house. He had taken off his suit and shirt and was wearing a simple kurta pajama. Under his arm he carried his suit and shirt, carefully folded so that they would stay fresh.

The next day I stood bravely by his door while others went into his office and left. Finally he looked up. "Why are you staring at me, girl? What do you want?"

I crept into his office and stood respectfully at his desk. "Sir, my sass brought me here to sign some papers to say I was a widow and to get a pension."

"Yes," he said impatiently, "what of that? Are you not getting your pension?"

"My sass is getting it. She takes the envelope."

He frowned. "How that is arranged in your family is not for me to say. The pension comes. That is all that concerns this office."

"What if I came here each month to your office and the pension were to be handed to me?"

"Certainly not. That is not how it is done. The pension is mailed."

I took a deep breath. "What if I moved to another place?"

"Have you come here to tell me you are moving?"

"No, sir. I only want to know what would happen if I did."

"You are wasting my time with 'if, if, if.'"

"Please, just tell me. What would happen if I moved away?"

"Then you must go to the office in that new place and tell them you are there."

"And the pension would come to me there?"

"Yes, yes, yes. Now leave me in peace."

I hurried back through the marketplace, past the man with the trained monkey on a chain and the stall where birds were imprisoned in tiny cages. In one of the cages was a mynah bird that had been blinded to make it sing. I shuddered, feeling no better off than the chained monkey and the miserable birds. I knew I had to find a way to escape. I could write to my maa and baap, but what could I say that would not bring shame and sorrow to them?

I began to make plans. I doubted that I could live on the pension alone, but my silver earrings would help until I could find a job of some sort. But who would hire me? In the city I would be seen as the poor country girl I was, shrouded in a widow's sari and with no proper schooling. And where would I live? How long would the money from my earrings last? With all these questions I did not think to run away today or tomorrow, but as long as I had the thought of someday, I could stand

Sass's scolding. To leave would take courage, and of that I did not have much.

As long as I stayed with my sass and sassur, I at least had a place to sleep and food to eat, though food seemed to be getting scarcer. As Sassur ate less, Sass became more stingy. She kept the keys to the cupboard knotted in her sari, all but counting the grains of rice. Some days I was so hungry, I felt dizzy. Worse than my hunger was the lack of happiness in the house. Even the bandicoot sensed it. After a while he would no longer come out from under the veranda, even for the bit of food I could spare him.

Then suddenly my world changed once more. Late in the afternoon of a day when the sun was like a circle of fire in the sky, Sassur came home early from school. This had never happened before. He went into his room and lay down on his charpoy. Minutes later I heard Sass screaming. Sassur had quietly died.

s e v e n

Chandra was called home. It had been over a year since her wedding. She no longer looked like a young girl. She wore a handsome sari. It was white, out of respect for her father's death, but unlike my white sari, Chandra's was made of fine muslin. Her hair was caught up in a complicated twist, and there were gold bangles on her arms. And the toenails sticking out of her sandals were painted! After embracing her mother and shedding many tears, she put her arms around me. "Koly, how I have missed you. There is no time now, but tonight after the funeral we'll talk the sun up."

This time there was no money for a funeral in Varanasi. Sassur's thumbs were tied together to show that he could no longer work, and his big toes were also tied together so that his ghost could not return. He was carried on his charpoy to an empty place in one of the fields to be cremated. As I watched, I thought of how he had said, "One day I will walk off across the fields, and you will see no more of me."

Three fires were lit nearby, and the men of the town chanted during the cremation until his spirit had left his body and a holy man announced that Sassur was dead.

After the funeral, as we walked back to the house, each of us was given seven pebbles. We had to drop the small stones, one by one. It is known that a spirit is poor at counting but loves to count anyhow. Sassur's spirit would occupy itself with counting the pebbles and would not follow us home. I whispered to Chandra as we dropped our tiny stones that I did not believe her baap would wish to return.

Chandra had been lucky. That night as we sat up and talked, she told me of her new life. "My sass is not well and spends her day lying on her charpoy in the courtyard talking with her friends about her poor health. Each day she has a new symptom. The running of the house is left to me with no interference, and there is a servant to help with the hard work. We had electricity put into the house so that my husband could bring home a computer from his workplace. He sits before it and touches the keys, and he can make colored pictures." She looked shyly at me. "Koly, if only I had listened to you and learned to read, I could know some of what comes up on the screen. There are words in every language and from everywhere. My baap was wrong to dislike those machines. They are magic.

"And because of the electricity we have a television. You remember how we went to the village to see the television? But there my baap was right. Such things you see on the American programs! Very improper!" She whispered what some of the things were, and we giggled until Sass poked her head into our room to shame us, reminding us that a funeral had taken place that day.

In the three days we had together, Chandra was treated as a guest. While I went about my usual tasks, she spent most of the day in the courtyard with Sass, so Sass could brag about Chandra's good fortune to the neighbor women. It was only in the evenings that we could whisper to each other. I told her how I had talked with the man in the village about my pension. "One day I will run away," I said.

"No. You must never do that. Where would you go, and who would take care of you?"

I knew that Chandra was never one to think of taking care of herself, so I said no more. Still, seeing how happy she was, I began to think more often of whether one day I might be happy as well.

At the end of the week Chandra returned to her husband's home and our life went on, but without Sassur nothing was the same. Sass did not even have the energy to scold me when I let the ghee boil over into the fire or forgot to sweep the courtyard. As the months went by, her sad moods drove away her friends, and the courtyard was now empty in the afternoons. She sat all day long staring at nothing. Her hair was untidy and her sari soiled. Often I caught her looking at me in a strange way.

I was sorry for her. We might have been a comfort to each other, and once I even said, "Now we are both widows."

Sass drew herself up. "What do you say? Do you have a daughter who has married well? Or a son who died in the holy city of Varanasi? We are not the same."

After Sassur's death there was no more money coming from the school. Her widow's pension hardly bought our food. The brass bowls, Sass's best sari, and her silver bangles were all carried to the moneylender in the village. On the days Sass returned from the moneylender, she would stare and stare at me. I tried to keep out of her sight and to eat as little as possible, but I think if she could have snapped her fingers and made me disappear, I would surely have been gone.

Often she asked about my silver earrings, still sure I had hidden them. I only shook my head. I tried to be as silent and invisible as the little chameleons in the courtyard, but when I saw her take down Sassur's book of Tagore's poems with his signature, I begged her not to sell it.

"We cannot eat the book, and the moneylender will give me a good sum. My husband always said it was valuable." She wrapped the book carelessly in a bit of cloth and set off for the village. I stood in the road and watched until I could bear it no longer. I ran after her, my feet sending up little clouds of dust.

"If I find my silver earrings and give them to you, will you give me the book?" I asked.

Sass's eyes flashed. "So you have lied to me all along!" she screeched. Then she thrust the book at me. "Take it and give me the earrings at once."

As soon as I pried out the brick and held the earrings in my hand, I saw what a foolish thing I had done, but it was too late. I knew I could not bear to see the book that meant so much to Sassur sold. So it was my earrings that Sass carried to the village to sell, and with them my last hope.

One day a letter came. Sass would not show it to me but took it to the village for the scribe to read to her. When she returned, Sass was smiling. "It is from my younger brother. He lives in Delhi, and he will take me in. He says he needs someone to look after his children and help with the housework."

In a small voice I asked, "What will happen to me?"

Sass gave me a sly look. "Oh, you will come as well. No doubt he will find something for you to do. Now I must sell the cow and the house to get money for our trip."

The house with its melting mud walls and skimpy square of land brought little. Sass did better with the cow, but I was sorry to see her go, for many times when I had milked her, I had whispered my worries to her. I helped to drive the cow to the village, but when it came time for Sass to buy the railway tickets, she sent me home. "There is no need for you to come along," she said.

When Sass returned, the tickets were quickly put away. Sass appeared almost happy, pulling out the few remaining pots to make pooris, which we had not had since Chandra's marriage. "I have an appetite," she said. And then she added, with the same sly smile I had seen so much lately, "I have a treat for you. We will stop at Vrindavan on our way to Delhi. It is a holy city with a great many temples. It would be well for us to make a pilgrimage before beginning our new lives."

I was excited at the thought of seeing such a holy city, but puzzled. Never before had my sass spoken of temples. She seldom started her day with a puja to the household shrine. Perhaps, I thought, Sassur's death has made her think more about such things. Still, I was uncertain.

As unhappy as I had been in my sass's house, a thorn of sadness pricked at me when it came time to leave. I had swept the courtyard so often that every inch was familiar to me. There was the mango tree with the rope Chandra and I had swung on. There was the little garden where I brought water to the neat rows of eggplant and okra. The river where I washed the clothes and studied my books was a friend. I could not guess how it would be to live in a large city like Delhi. I did not know how the family of Sass's brother would treat me. Because I was leaving it, my sass's house, where for so long I had felt unwelcome, now seemed like home. I even said good-bye to the bandicoot, which switched its tail and twitched its whiskers at me in a friendly way.

Sass said good-bye to nothing and counted the hours until our departure. She hummed as she packed her things. I was pleased to see she took the quilt I had made in Hari's memory.

The morning we were to leave, she was up before dawn, a greedy smile on her face as if she were about to take a big bite of something tasty. I made a bedroll of the quilt I had made for my dowry. My few clothes and my book of Tagore's poems went into a basket. We set out in a wagon for the railway station. I kept looking back over my shoulder at what had been our home, but Sass stared straight ahead.

At the station we pushed our way through the crowds and past water wallahs, tea wallahs, and ice cream wallahs. Sass paused only to buy two palm leaf fans, giving me one. I took it gratefully. It was the only gift she had ever given to me.

By the time we struggled into the ladies' compartment of the train, all the seats were taken. We had to push our way onto a little space of floor. It was hot and smelly, and I couldn't move without getting in the way of someone else. Still, my unhappiness and worry soon melted into wonder as miles of green fields rushed by, and small villages, and once a large city.

More people crowded onto the train, so I was pushed into a corner where I could no longer look out or feel the slight breeze from the open window. Most of the passengers, like ourselves, had brought something to eat for the journey. The smells of the food, along with the swaying and jerks of the train, were beginning to make me sick.

Sass studied me. "You're pale, girl; you had better get out at the next stop and take some air." At the next stop, with much complaining, Sass led me off the train. She opened her umbrella to shield us from the hot sun and walked me about. When we got back on the train, I finally fell asleep.

When I awoke, we had reached the holy city of Vrindavan. As we got off the train and I saw the crowds of people, I asked, "Where will we stay, Sass?"

"I'll find a place," she said. "For now we'll leave our things at the parcel office so we won't have to carry them about."

After we checked our baskets and bedrolls, Sass handed me my claim check and hurried me into the street, where she hailed a bicycle rickshaw. The rickshaw was decorated with small flags in bright colors. The seats were swept clean and the bicycle polished. "Take us to a temple," Sass ordered the rickshaw boy.

The boy laughed. "There are four thousand temples. Which one do you want?" The boy was only a few years older than I was. He was tall and lean, but in the leanness there was strength. His hair was badly cut and stood up in odd tufts. There was an insolent look on his face. I admired him for not being intimidated by my sass. "Make up your minds," he told us. "I'm losing money by standing here."

Sass gave him a push. "Don't be rude with me,

boy. Just take us to a temple. Any temple." She gave the boy a shrewd look. "One close by. I'm not going to pay a big fare." She climbed into the rickshaw and pulled me in after her.

The boy shrugged and, standing on the pedals to give himself a start, he took off. As we rode through the streets of the city, everywhere I looked I saw women in white widows' saris like mine. "Why are there so many widows here, Sass?" I asked.

She shrugged. "It is the city they come to. They are taken care of here."

Many of the widows were old, but many were young, some even younger than I was. Suddenly I was anxious to leave the city. "How long will we stay here, Sass?" I asked.

"Only a day."

I breathed a sigh of relief. However difficult my life would be in Delhi, I would not be surrounded by thousands of widows to remind me that my life, like theirs, was over.

The boy stopped his rickshaw and held out his hand. "Four rupees," he demanded.

Sass glared at him. "You take us for country folk who know no better? Two rupees is enough." The boy ran after us complaining so loudly that Sass grudgingly gave him the other two rupees. As he turned away, he gave me an impudent wink.

The temple was filled with chanting widows in white saris. Some looked peaceful, almost joyful. Others looked thin, hungry, and miserable, as if they wished they were somewhere else. Their hunger reminded me of my own. Our food on the train had lasted only until breakfast. As if she could read my mind, Sass said, "Here is a fifty-rupee note. Go and find us some food, and don't settle for the first vendor you see. I'll wait in the temple where it's cool. Mind you don't lose the change."

I clasped the money tightly in my hand, afraid someone would take it from me. Sass had never before trusted me with so much money. Keeping my eye on the temple to be sure I would not be lost, I went by two vendors before I found one with samosas that looked both clean and tasty. I asked the price and counted my change twice. Holding two samosas in one hand and the rupees I had received in change in the other, I hurried back to the corner of the temple where I had left Sass. She wasn't there. While I waited for her to return, I ate my samosa. I could not imagine where she had gone. Finally I decided she was looking for a place for us to stay. Still, I felt little shivers of fear.

I tried not to worry. The temple was cool and the sound of the chanting peaceful. Now that my stomach was satisfied, I felt a little better. I waited for an hour and then another hour. The chanting never stopped. Somehow I believed that as long as the chanting went on, I had nothing to worry about. It would only be a matter of time before Sass would return for me and all would be well. It was nearly dusk when the chanting stopped. The second samosa had been eaten long ago. The widows in their white saris stole silently from the temple. A terrible panic came over me. I rushed from the temple.

I didn't know where to start looking for Sass. I was used to our small village. The streets of

Vrindavan were like an overturned ants' nest. I wondered if I had misheard Sass. Perhaps she had changed her mind about staying in Vrindavan. Maybe she had told me to meet her back at the railway station. I stopped one of the widows and asked for directions to the station. She looked at my white widow's sari. I thought I saw in her look pity, and something more frightening—a look of kinship.

Though the sun was setting, it was still hot, as if some invisible sun were beating down on me. Beads of perspiration formed on my forehead and my upper lip and ran down my face. My sari clung to me. Shops and businesses were closing, and the streets became moving rivers of people pushing against one another.

Twice more I had to stop someone to ask directions. Each time there was a pitying look on the face of the widow I asked. It was nearly dark when I finally arrived at the station, where passengers waiting for the morning trains were cooking their suppers on small stoves. Some were already stretched out on mats. I quickly made the rounds of the station, but Sass was not there.

I went to the parcel counter where we had checked our things and got my basket and bedroll. "Did the woman who was with me come for her things?" I asked, but the attendant had just come on duty and knew nothing of Sass.

At the entrance to the station stood a line of rickshaws. I had forty-seven rupees tied up in my sari, but I could not waste them on a rickshaw, and anyhow I would not know where to go. In the line I saw a rickshaw with small flags, and next to it stood the boy with the wayward hair. I felt a great relief in seeing someone in the city I had seen before, someone I almost knew. I hurried toward him. "Have you seen my sass?" I asked.

He stared at me for a long while as if he were trying to remember me. "Oh, yes," he said with a bitter smile. "I was back here when she returned. She tried to cheat her new driver just as she cheated me."

"If she came back, where is she now?"

"On the train. I saw her get on the train to Delhi. It wasn't an hour after I had taken you to the temple."

eight

I suppose part of me had known all along. The thought had been waiting like a scorpion at the edge of my mind. Now it stung me, and I nearly cried out with the pain. There had been the letters from her brother in Delhi that she had never let me see. There had been the secret buying of the railway tickets. There had been the mysterious smile. She had taken care that I did not know her address in Delhi. I knew I could never find her in that city of millions. All I had were the forty-seven rupees tied into my sari. I understood now why she had entrusted me with so much money. It was to ease her conscience. Much as I hated to let the boy see me weep, I could not keep tears from streaming down my cheeks.

The boy looked at me. "It happens every day here," he said. "You can go and chant in the temple like the other widows do. The monks will give you food."

He continued to look at me. The insolent look was gone, and there was kindness in his face. He was about to say something when a man with a briefcase jumped into his rickshaw and ordered, "Get along." The boy gave me one more look and pedaled away.

It was evening. The shadows climbed up the walls of the jumbled buildings and fell across the narrow alleys. I walked aimlessly. One street looked like another, and I could not tell if I had been down them before. I didn't know what I was looking for, only that I hadn't found it and didn't think I ever would. My bedroll and basket were heavy. I was tired and hungry and only wanted to lie down. I knew others must have felt the same, for charpoys and mattresses began to appear on the sidewalks. Sometimes one person, sometimes a whole family settled down to sleep. I would have welcomed dropping down on a bit of sidewalk, but I didn't know what was allowed or what bit of sidewalk was spoken for.

An elderly woman was watching me from a doorstep where she huddled, her dirty white widow's sari drawn about her. She beckoned to me with a long, bony finger. When I went over to her, she moved even further into the corner of the doorway. She pointed to the empty space she had made. "You can sleep here," she said. "The people in the house will not chase you away. They even threw out a little food for me." She handed me a small portion of rice. It was cold and sticky. Gratefully I swallowed it. "Have you just come?" she asked.

"Yes, my sass left me this morning. I don't know where she is. Maybe she will come back for me."

The old woman shook her head. "You won't see her again. It was the same with me. I came two months ago. When my husband died, I was no longer needed. His property was divided between his brothers. The brothers brought me here."

"Why would they bring you here and leave

you?" I asked. "Why didn't they take care of you?"

"Once they had my husband's property, they had no more use for me. They said widows were unlucky to have about. The truth is that I am too old for hard work."

If there were such cruelness in the world, then it might indeed be true that Sass had taken me to this place of widows just to get rid of me. I was alone in a strange city with only a few rupees and no friends. "How do you get by?" I managed to ask.

"I am a servant of the Lord Krishna. Like the other widows I go each day to a temple and chant for four hours. The monks in the temple feed us, and there is the pittance of my widow's pension. I had a room I shared with other widows, but the landlord wanted it back for his family, so we were all turned out. Now I must find a new room."

All around us people were settling down on the sidewalks. Babies and small children snuggled against their mothers or sisters. Some of the people fell asleep immediately, as if their square of sidewalk were as much a shelter as a house would be.

Others chatted with their neighbors or prepared a bit of food, feeding the cooking fires with leaves and twigs. Across from us small children were pushing dogs aside to hunt for bits of food in a pile of rubbish.

Even with my bedroll to soften the stone of the doorway, I could not sleep. Often I reached down to assure myself that the rupees were still tied carefully in a corner of my sari and then tucked securely into my waist knot. I told myself I should see if the rupees would buy a railway or bus ticket back to my maa and baap. But how could I do that? What the woman had told me was true. Because they had lost their husbands, widows were considered unlucky. If my family learned what had happened to me, it would bring them unhappiness and even shame. By now my older brother might be married, and his wife would be living in the home of my parents. There would be no room for me. Somehow I would have to make my life here.

The next morning I was awakened by the chanting of morning hymns coming over loudspeakers. The widow I had shared the doorstep with was gone. The mattresses and charpoys were disappearing from the sidewalks. At a street corner I joined a line at a faucet for a little water to wash in and to drink. I bought the cheapest bowl of dal I could find.

I could not keep myself from returning to the railway station. I did not really believe I would ever see Sass again; still, I could not help hoping that she would come back. I waited all day. Once I saw a woman in the distance who I thought was Sass. I called out and ran toward her, only to find a stranger, annoyed by my cries. Even the rickshaw boy did not appear.

That night I had the doorstep to myself, for the widow did not return. Just as she said, the door to the house opened and a bit of food was handed out, this time a chapati, which I quickly ate though a small child stood nearby watching hungrily. Afterward I was ashamed, for I still had some rupees, and the child had nothing.

I knew that I could not afford a room, but wandering through the city I saw signs tacked to some houses, advertising beds. When I inquired, I learned that if I were to pay for both food and a bed, my rupees would soon be gone. After asking several widows, I found the government building where pensions were given out. There was a form to be filled out. Because of Sassur's teaching I was able quickly to complete the form, all but an address. I could not say I lived on a doorstep off the Purana Bazaar.

"You have not put your address down," the official said.

"Until I get my pension," I explained, "I can't afford a place to live. Can't I pick up my pension here?"

He shook his head as if the thought were beyond considering. "No, no. Pensions are mailed. Return when you have an address."

I tried everywhere to find work, but for every job there were a hundred seekers. For a week the doorstep was my home. When others tried to sleep there, I was not as generous as the elderly widow had been but selfishly chased them away. My rupees were nearly gone, and all I had was the doorstep and the bit of food tossed out to me by the hand of someone I had never seen. I would fight for the doorstep rather than give it up, but I knew that my hunger and my fear were making me into another person altogether, a greedy and coldhearted person I despised. I thought it would be Sass's final cruelty to me, to make me be like her.

I visited the temples: the Govindji, with its great hall and its row of columns like tree trunks and its high ceilings where neat rows of bats hung like small furry pennants. I went to the Banke Bihari, where there was a darshan each day—the curtains were opened for a moment to give a glimpse of the deity, which is a great blessing. In all the temples, I saw the widows chanting hour after hour. I admired their piety and envied the food the monks gave them in return for their devotions, but try as I might, after only a half hour of chanting, my mind wandered. I could hardly breathe for the smell of incense and the mustard oil burning in the hundreds of little lamps. I found myself stealing away from the temple, relieved to be out in the open air.

I made my way through the bazaars and along the ghats of the Yamuna River, lost among all the pilgrims to the city. Each afternoon I returned to the railway station, not from any hope but out of habit and because it had become familiar. On the day I had spent my last rupee and thought that I must sell Tagore's book, I saw the boy with the rickshaw again. I tried to get his attention. Thousands of people had hurried by me without so much as a glance. I longed to exchange a word with someone who recognized me.

At first he had eyes only for the passengers who had just gotten off a train. When no one climbed into his rickshaw, he squatted down, waiting for his next chance. Hesitantly I went over to him. He gave me a quizzical look. I guessed how untidy and dirty I must appear after a week of sleeping on the doorstop. "You still here?" he asked, but not unkindly. "I've seen you before. When are you going to give up coming to the station?"

"I have no other place to go."

"Well, you shouldn't stay here. There are bad

people about this station who look for young girls from the country."

I could not keep from telling him my worries. "I am tired of sleeping in the street, and my rupees are all gone." I bit my lip to keep from crying.

He looked at me. "Don't blubber. I'll show you a place to go. You have to wait until I have finished work. Sit over there, and I'll come back for you." He called to a family who had just left an incoming train. After bartering with him, they climbed onto his rickshaw, and he pedaled away.

As it grew dark, people began to look for places to lie down for the night. I saw a man in blue jeans and a red shirt staring at me. I huddled into a corner of the station, trying to make myself as inconspicuous as possible. After a bit he came over to me. Bristly hair stuck out of his cheeks and chin. When he smiled at me, I saw that most of his teeth were missing. When he spoke to me, his voice was pleasant enough, but he had about him the smell of a hungry dog. "A refined girl like you," he said, "should not have to sleep in the streets. If you come with me, I will find a proper place for you where there is plenty of food." I thought of what the rickshaw boy had said about bad people. I drew myself further into my corner, trying to escape the man.

Still he hovered over me like a bat. "It is a waste for such a pretty girl to dress in a widow's sari. I have a sari with real gold threads. It would make me very happy to see you wear it." He reached down and took my arm and jerked me to my feet. Terrified, I pulled away, but he was too strong for me. I looked about, hoping to find someone to help me, but the crowds were so great, no one was paying attention. I thought of the dog's grip on the gosling's neck and knew I must not let him take me. I sank my teeth into the man's arm, making him howl in surprise and pain. He slapped me and ran off.

For safety I settled near a family of a maa and baap and their three children. They were waiting for a seat on the early-morning train, they said, and would be there all night. It hurt to see the way they laughed and played with their little ones. It was so long ago when I was small and a part of a happy family.

I did not have much faith that the rickshaw boy would return. Like Sass, he was probably trying to get rid of me with his promise. It was growing late, and by now someone else would have claimed my doorstep. In the morning, I decided, I would go to the temple. I would chant all day to show how holy I was, and the monks would keep me from starving. At least in the temple I would be safe from evil men. I would become one of the thousands of widows of Vrindavan. That would be my life for as long as I lived.

When at last the boy returned, he said "You can get into the rickshaw now."

"I have no money left to pay you."

"That's all right. The man I work for won't know. I pedaled fast all evening so I could report enough rides to cover this time, but hurry. In a few minutes I have to turn the rickshaw in."

"You don't own it?"

"How could I own such a thing? A man hires me and pays me a percentage of my earnings. It buys me food and the corner of a room I share with some other boys."

"Why don't you ask for more money?"

"The owner of the rickshaw would fire me and give my job to another boy. There are boys coming in from the countryside every day in search of work. Still, as little as the money is, I spend only half of it."

"You spend only half? What do you do with the other half?"

"I own land," he said. A smile grew on his face. "It was left to me by my father. My uncle cares for it. When I have enough money for seeds and irrigation, I'm going back to my village. I hate this city." Perhaps it was because it was the end of the day, but he seemed not to have much strength left for the pedaling. In the dark I could just make out white shapes like ghosts huddled in doorways and curled against buildings. "There are so many widows," I whispered.

"Yes," the boy said, a little out of breath. "Families bring them here from all over India. They are left just as your sass left you. Only if you ask me, you're lucky to be rid of her."

It was true that Sass had often scolded me. She

had left me alone in this city as if she were dropping a kitten down a well. Still, I would have given anything to be back in the village, safe behind the walls of a house, even if it meant spending the rest of my life being scolded by Sass.

We rounded a corner and turned into a small courtyard where several women were gathered, some as young as I was. An older woman came toward us. She was very plump, as though she had been put together with pillows. Even the many meters of her sari barely stretched around her. "Raji," she called to the boy, "have you brought me another? There is no room! Never mind, we will manage. What is your name, girl?"

"Koly," I whispered. I put my hands together and bowed.

"I am Kamala, but here everyone calls me Maa Kamala. Go away now, Raji—you have no business in the courtyard with the girls. But wait, first take some of this curd and cucumber to fill your stomach. You are looking thinner than ever. It will do you no good to save money by going without food.

You will be too weak to pedal your rickshaw."

She turned to me. "Come along, Koly," she said in a brisk voice. "I'll introduce you to the others. Then we must put aside that widow's sari. Here you are not a widow but a young woman with a life ahead of you."

The others looked at me with curiosity. "Where do you come from?" one of them asked. I named our village. "I never heard of it," she said. "You must be a country girl. You'll have much to learn if you stay in this city."

"Tanu," Maa Kamala scolded, "what kind of welcome is that? Were you so rudely greeted when you came? I think not. Show a little kindness. Take Koly inside and find her something to wear from the clothes in the chest."

Tanu led me into a small room off the courtyard. She was eighteen, a year older than I was, and much more sophisticated. She wore dark lipstick, and her eyelashes were heavy with mascara. She was tall, with long, narrow feet and hands. Her hands had a strange orange color and she had a distinct smell, not unpleasant but very strong. She threw open a chest and pulled out some clothes, flinging a pair of trousers and a tunic at me. "These look your size. Put them on."

I slipped the trousers on under my sari, and then, as my sari came off, I hastily pulled on the tunic. Taking off my widow's sari was a great relief. I once saw a small green snake rub itself against a stone until its old skin peeled away, transparent and thin as paper. I felt now as I imagined the snake felt after it rid itself of its old, confining skin.

"Much better," Tanu said. She smiled in approval.

"What kind of place is this?" I asked, lowering my voice.

"A widows' house," Tanu said. "Maa Kamala takes in widows off the street and finds us jobs. She helps us get our widow's pension and lets us stay here until we can support ourselves. Someday I hope to be earning enough to share a room with some other girls and live on my own. Maa Kamala is nice, but she is very strict."

"Where does Maa Kamala get the money to take in so many girls? There must be twenty out there in the courtyard."

"A rich lady from the town supports the house, and we pay a little for our room and board from our wages."

"How did you come here?" I asked.

"I ran away when I heard my sass and sassur plotting to get rid of me so my husband could marry again and get another dowry."

"How could people be so cruel!" I was horrified.

"What about you?" she asked.

"My husband died. I was brought here by my sass after she became a widow and was going to her brother's house, where I was not wanted."

That night in the courtyard I heard many stories like mine and many stories like Tanu's. Hearing so many frightening stories made me feel less sorry for myself.

At last Maa Kamala threw up her arms and ordered us to stop. "Enough of your miserable tales," she said. "You wallow like pigs in mud. That is all in the past. Now, Koly, we must find you a job. Nearby in the bazaar is a man who furnishes all that is needed for ceremonies. Tanu works there stringing marigold garlands. The man is looking for another girl. I warn you, the hours are long and you have to be fast. What do you say?"

I could not stop myself. For an answer I put my arms around as much of Maa Kamala as I could reach and hugged her.

nine

That night, for the first time since coming to Vrindavan, I felt safe. Lying nearby were other widows, their soft sighs and turnings like so many doves fluttering around me. I tried not to think what would have happened to me if I had not found Raji. No one was more fortunate than I.

Early in the morning Maa Kamala stirred us up like a pot of rice. "Hurry, hurry," she called. "You must not be late for your work." We quickly washed beside the courtyard faucet and swallowed some dal. Chapatis were given out, and we were shooed like chickens from the courtyard out into the city.

"You will work with Tanu, in the same stall,"

Maa Kamala said. "She will show you the way. And here is money for your lunch."

Together Tanu and I hurried down the streets. We had to pick our way over sleeping bodies. Whole households of baaps, maas, and children lay on their charpoys or on the sidewalk. On the way to the bazaar we passed the doorway where I had spent my nights. Another widow was curled up there, still asleep. I shivered at the sight and gave thanks for a roof over my head. As I hurried by, I looked for the half-starved child who had stood there watching me eat. I still held my breakfast chapati and would gladly have given it to her. There were children there, but she was not among them. I could not put her hungry stare out of my head, and my happiness dwindled a little.

The early-morning streets were crowded with cars and bicycles and rickshaws and oxcarts. Here and there a cow wandered in and out of the road, bringing the traffic to a halt. In the bazaar the booths were already open. We passed leather workers and pillow shops and booths where brass vases and pots were for sale. There was a booth that sold bangles and another with bolts of brightly colored cloth for saris. There were stalls with rugs and stalls with heaps of spices: gold turmeric and precious orange saffron.

Tanu pulled me after her. "If we are late, Mr. Govind will be cross all day and will give us no time for our lunch."

As we entered the booth, Mr. Govind, a small man with flowing mustaches, was shouting at two women seated on the floor surrounded by a pile of marigold blossoms. "No gossiping," he ordered. "We have three funerals and two marriages." He gave me a quick look. "You are the new girl? Tanu will show you what to do. I hope you will learn fast. I can't pay someone who is slow and clumsy. Quick now, girls."

We were surrounded with heaps of orange flowers. The smell of the marigolds was so strong, I could hardly breathe. Now I knew what Tanu smelled like. It was the spicy, sharp odor of the marigolds. "You'll get used to it," Tanu said when she saw me sniffing. "Here is how it is done." The flower heads had already been snapped from the stems. She showed me how long fibers from banana stems were soaked in water to soften them. "The flower is threaded onto the fiber and caught in a knot like this. Then the next flower is slipped on. You are not to put the flowers too close together. That uses too many of them."

I watched for a minute or two and then began to thread the flowers. Tanu and the other two women worked twice as fast as I did. If I tried to hurry, the flowers dropped off the fiber, but the work was simple, and I soon caught on. By lunchtime I was knotting the garlands into neat circles and tossing them onto the heap of garlands as quickly as Tanu and the others. Once or twice Mr. Govind came by to see how I was doing. He must have been satisfied; he allowed us twenty minutes to eat our lunch.

Tanu and I wandered through the marketplace admiring the cinema posters with pictures of glamorous women and handsome men. In the mirror booth we stopped to look at ourselves. Keeping an eye on the clock, we bought a little pot of vegetables and rice. We ate quickly and then wandered by a perfume stall that smelled deliciously of sandalwood. We stopped at the bangle booth. We tried on so many of the brightly colored glass bangles that the owner complained, "You are keeping my customers away. Come back when you have some money." He smiled at us. "You make the marigold garlands?" He was looking at our orange hands. "Could you string beads?"

Eagerly we said we could.

"Stop by tomorrow. I'll talk with Govind. If he tells me you are good girls, maybe I will give you some beads to take home to make into bangles. If you make them well, I'll give you one. Now off with you."

Giggling, we hurried back to the stall, planning all the while what colored beads we wanted for our own bangles. We found Mr. Govind beating his fists against the wall and moaning, "They have sent jasmine blossoms instead of marigolds! We will be short for the wedding!"

Tanu whispered, "It is always a crisis with him. Pay no attention."

But I felt sorry for him. "Couldn't we make some garlands from the jasmine?" I asked Mr. Govind.

"Not traditional. We must have marigolds."

"What if we mixed the flowers? It would stretch them out, and there would still be marigolds on each one."

He looked worried. Finally he said, "It is all we can do."

When the family came for the garlands, they complimented Mr. Govind. "Something new, something different," they said. "Our guests will be impressed."

After that Mr. Govind must have spoken well of us to the bangle maker. The next day, at lunchtime, the bangle man gave us a bag of beads and a spool of wire. He showed us how to fasten the bangle after it was finished and warned us, "I have counted every bead. There had better be the right amount on the bracelets, or you will pay for each one that is missing."

The girls at Maa Kamala's were envious of our work. To pacify them, we let them try on the finished bangles. Each evening we sat cross-legged in the courtyard threading beads in the last light of the day. When it was dark, we went inside and kept threading, stopping only to hunt for any beads that slipped away. By the end of the week Tanu and I each had our own bangle. Tanu would have gone on until she had an armful of bangles, but I soon grew bored with the work. Unlike my embroidery, which came from my head and heart, the threading of tiny glass beads grew tiresome.

Tanu and I became good friends. We shared a room with three other widows, two of them much older than we were. They said bangles on the arm of a widow were unseemly and grew impatient with our staying up late and giggling, which kept them awake. Our room was very plain, so I hung my dowry quilt on one of the walls to make the room more cheerful. There was my maa in her green sari and my baap on his bicycle. There were my brothers playing at soccer and our courtyard with its tamarind tree and me at the well. After a while I stopped looking at the quilt, for it made me very homesick.

Half of our wages went to pay our expenses at the widows' house, and the rest was put aside for us. Each week Maa Kamala made a note in a little book of what was saved from the wages. My savings were not much, but each week they grew. Early one morning I went to apply for my pension. This time I proudly filled in the form myself, giving an address and signing my name. Soon the envelope with my pension came, and the pension was added to my savings. I saw that though it would be a while, the day might come when I could move from the widows' house to make room for another widow. Tanu and I even talked of a time when we might share a room.

Now that we were no longer stringing beads, I entertained Tanu after supper by reading Tagore's poems aloud, although the older widows said I would have done better to read the sacred verses. Tanu loved to hear the poems, and after a bit even the widows who had disapproved of them began to listen. Everyone had her favorite; the older widows asked for the poems about the sadness of life and the younger ones for the poems about love.

One evening Raji came to the courtyard while I was reading the poem about the homeless bird. He sat in the far corner of the courtyard munching some leftovers Maa had given him and listening to the poem, a dreamy expression on his face. He seemed to get such pleasure from it that I handed Raji the book and asked him if he would like to read some of the poems.

He shook his head. From the embarrassed look on his face I guessed why and blurted out, "Can't you read?"

Angrily he snapped at me, "How could I read when I was working on the land from the time I was five years old? Besides, there is no one in my family who reads. Who would teach me?"

I took a deep breath and asked, "Would you like me to teach you?" I was grateful to Raji for all he had done for me and was anxious for a chance to do something for him in exchange.

Raji kicked at the dust and glowered at me. At last he shrugged and agreed.

Each evening I would return to Maa Kamala's house exhausted, the scent of marigolds hanging over me like a cloud. I would join the other widows for a dinner of curried lentils or rice, sometimes with a bit of fish or some morsels of chicken. At dusk Raji would appear, tired and cross and half starved, for he was counting every rupee until he had enough to return to his farm. Maa Kamala would give him something to eat, and after a bit, as his stomach filled, he would stop snapping at me. At first he was impatient, but as the letters became words, and the words thoughts, he became both eager and suspicious, as though I were holding something back from him. Soon he took the book in his own hands and, moving his finger slowly, read the words by himself.

He did not like to have the other widows see him struggling with his reading, so we sat in a corner of the courtyard with only Maa Kamala to keep an eye on us. I began to look forward to Raji's visits. I would steal a glance at him as he read out the words of the poems. His tousled hair fell over his forehead, and sometimes, when the lesson was too long and Raji was too tired, his long lashes would flutter as he tried to keep from falling asleep. His hands on the book were the strong hands of a man who has worked all his life, but his hold on the book was a gentle one.

When his day had been successful and he had received generous tips, he would bring me some little thing, a paper of sugared almonds spiced with pepper and cumin, and once a handful of lilies, which he wound in my hair while I put one behind his ear. I would tell Raji about the girls I worked with, and he would tell me about the people he had carried that day. Raji was the only one to whom I could complain, confiding in him that I was afraid I would have to spend the rest of my life in a sea of orange marigolds. After a day when he had few customers and no tips, Raji would have no heart for books, but most of the time he was eager to learn.

His favorite poems were those that described the countryside, poems about being out early when the morning light is thin and pale, and about hearing the birds' songs. "Your poet must have spent time in a village like mine," he said. "I count the days until I can return there."

"Don't you like the city, Raji?" I asked.

"I hate its crowds and misery. In the countryside around our village it is easy to find a place where there is not another human being. I can go to that place, and my thoughts will not be all tangled with the thoughts of other people."

"I know what you mean," I said. I told him about the river where I had washed the clothes among the kingfishers and the dragonflies, and the calls of the doves and the wind rustling through the leaves of the peepul trees.

"I know of a place on the river I could show you," he said. There was an eagerness in his voice. "Tomorrow I'll come for you right after you eat. In only a half hour's walk the city disappears."

I agreed at once. I was happy at the thought of walking along the river, and I guessed Raji was anxious to give me some treat in return for my teaching.

The next evening I slipped away to meet Raji.

Maa Kamala was very proper and didn't approve of boys and girls mixing except under her watchful eye. Raji was waiting down the road for me. Work was over, and people had returned to their homes. Even the monks and widows in the temples were silent. The whole city seemed elsewhere. We hurried through the deserted streets and headed north along the river, Raji always a bit ahead of me and looking back to be sure I was following.

The breezes off the river were pleasant. We were outside the town's center now. Only a few people passed by, no one paying attention to us. A few fishermen were out in their boats. Two women at the river's edge were beating clothes against rocks while their children placed twigs and leaves on the water and watched as the current caught them up. I thought of the times Sass had sent me to do the laundry at the river, and how much happier I was now.

Raji pointed to a temple on a distant hill. "That's where we're headed," he said. He began to run. I raced after him. We arrived at the temple laughing and breathless.

The temple was deserted. Through the arched entrance I could see an image of Krishna. "What is he holding up?" I asked.

"The hill of Govardhan," Raji said. "It's a hill not far from here. Krishna saved the sixteen thousand milkmaids he had married and all their cows from drowning in a terrible thunderstorm. He lifted the Govardhan hill on his little finger to shelter them. But it's not just the temple I want to show you. Come this way."

He scrambled down the riverbank. "Here," he said. "Here is a place on the river like the one you told me about. Listen—instead of the noise of the city, you can hear the wind through the trees. And there." He pointed to a branch that stuck out over the river. "A kingfisher." His voice was proud, as if he had caused the bird to appear.

We took off our sandals and paddled our dusty feet in the cool water. As it edged down, the sun seemed to rest on the river. A frog poked its head up, blinked a few times, and disappeared. "It's so quiet," I said. "It's the first peaceful minute I've had since I came to the city."

Raji smiled. "Yes, in the city it is all push and shove." He gave me a long look. "Koly, I have nearly enough now to rebuild the house and buy what I need for crops. Soon I'll be back in my village."

I wanted to tell him that I would miss him, but I didn't think saying such a thing would be seemly. Instead I said, "You're lucky to be leaving the city where one day is like another and you hardly notice the weather. It's like living inside a glass bottle. You'll be happier on your farm."

"I'll work the farm, but I'll have to live with my uncle until I fix the house. It's fallen apart since my maa and baap died." He reached down and, picking up a handful of pebbles, began to pitch them into the river. "When the house is finished," he said in a low voice, "I'll want a wife."

I found nothing to say to that. It was only natural that Raji should want a wife, but his words silenced me. I could only think how lucky a woman would be to be married to Raji; he was so kind and clever. I imagined him together with his wife on their farm, and for a moment I felt as lonely as I had on my first night in Vrindavan.

I saw him steal a glance at me and look away. He kept flinging pebbles, sending up little explosions of water. The commotion startled a heron hunting frogs along the edge of the river. The heron flew up, his great wings beating as fast as my heart, and melted into the dusky sky. We watched until the bird disappeared.

It was growing late. The setting sun had turned the river a muddy gray. "I have to get back," I said. "It will be dark soon."

We returned to the the city talking of nothing more than a famous cinema actress who had just married, and the mosquito bites we got by the river.

After that several weeks went by, and though I was there in the courtyard each evening waiting to greet him, Raji did not return. I wondered if I had said something to anger him. I worried that he had already left for the country and I would never see him again. I tried not to think about him, telling myself that now that I had taught him to read, our meetings were over. Still, I could not help but wonder why he had not come to say good-bye. I tried to put Raji out of my mind, but my mind would not obey me.

One evening Maa Kamala announced that the rich lady who paid for our widows' house was coming to see us. Everything, including the court-yard, was given a thorough cleaning. We put about vases of flowers and dressed in our best clothes. Maa Kamala fried pumpkin pooris and made shi-kanji with sweetened lime juice and ginger juice and sent us out to the bazaar at the last minute to get ice cubes in a little plastic sack, admonishing us to hurry so the ice would not melt.

Just before the rich lady arrived, Maa Kamala lined us all up to see if we were presentable. Tanu was sent back to wipe off some of her lipstick and mascara. An elderly widow was told not to cover her face with her sari because the rich lady did not approve of that custom.

We all stared as Maa Kamala greeted the rich lady with a respectful namaskar. Most of the widows thought her a great disappointment. "A face plain as a clay saucer and no gold threads woven in her sari," Tanu whispered. "And where is her jewelry?"

Our visitor was an older woman with a shapeless figure and unadorned clothes, but as she stopped to greet each of us, she had some small pleasant thing to say. She spoke to us in a direct and open way, so we did not feel like poor widows. She smiled knowingly, and I believe she understood just what we were thinking—perhaps she was amused at how we puzzled over her simple appearance. As she moved closer to me, I saw what Tanu had not noticed. Though there were no gold or silver threads woven into her sari, she wore a sari of great rarity and beauty. It appeared simple, but I knew it was made of a handwoven cloth called king's muslin, the very best you could buy. My maa had pointed out to me just such a sari when we visited the shop where she took her work. Along the borders of the rich lady's sari were embroidered flurries of blossoms in pale yellows and pinks twined with green leaves. I could not take my eyes from the clever work. She must have noticed my wide-eyed stare, for when it was my turn to greet her, she paused to ask, "What is it you do?"

"I string marigold garlands in the bazaar, madam," I said.

"I am sure you make a very good job of it." She seemed to want to say more, but after a second or two she moved on to the next widow.

We all stood stiffly with our cups of shikanji while Maa Kamala made a polite speech about how well we were doing and how grateful we were for the rich lady's help.

To my dismay Maa Kamala called out, "Koly, Tanu, show Madam through the rooms." She turned to the rich lady. "I hope you will find everything in order."

The lady smiled and said, "If there is too much order, I will think I have caused a lot of trouble for everyone."

That made me feel better. I nudged Tanu, who seemed unable to move, and we began to lead the rich lady from room to room. Some of the rooms were brightened with artificial flowers, and gaudy scarves hung on the walls. Some rooms had pious pictures of Lord Krishna. In one room I had to kick a pair of dirty sandals under a charpoy. As she followed along, the lady asked where we had come from and whether we were content at Maa Kamala's house and what our plans were. Tanu was tongue-tied, but I could still remember my nights on the street and the man who had tried to take me away, and I told the rich lady about those things.

When she had heard my story, she put her hand softly on my arm. She looked as if some mournful tune had found its way into her head and she could not lose it. "Those of you here at Maa Kamala's house are so few, and in the city there are so many." She sighed. "I wish I might do more. Indeed I will try." She gave herself a little shake and, smiling again, said, "Have I seen all the rooms?"

"Not ours," Tanu bravely answered.

"Then you must show it to me."

As we walked into the room, Tanu and I looked

frantically about for any disorder. The rich lady noticed the copy of Tagore's poems beside my bed. "Ah," she said touching the book, "he is my favorite, too." She stopped to look at my quilt. For a long moment she was silent. "Whose is this?" she asked.

I was too shy to claim it. Tanu said, "Koly made it for her dowry."

The lady turned to me. "Tell me about this quilt you have embroidered. The clouds there—why have you put those in?"

"They are the shape of the clouds that gather in our village before the rains come. That's our market-place with the herb stalls and the barber and dentist and the man with the basket of cobras." When I noticed Tanu standing there staring at me, I suddenly realized I was talking too much, and I closed my mouth.

The rich lady said, "I remember that you mentioned working in the bazaar making garlands."

I nodded, wondering if there was something in the quilt she did not like, and I would lose my job and be thrown out of Maa Kamala's house.

"I know a maker of fine saris," she said, "who is anxious to find women who are skilled in embroidery. But he does not want women who merely copy what others have done. He wants women who have original ideas and who can translate those ideas into their work. He is looking for artists."

I did not know what that had to do with me, but the woman was looking at me as if she were waiting for me to say something, so I mumbled, "Such artists must be difficult to find."

The rich lady laughed. "Evidently not so difficult, for just now I have found one! Tomorrow I will come and take you to see him."

t e n

The next day as I waited nervously, I asked Maa Kamala about the rich lady. Maa only shook her head and said, "You must not call her that. She has a name like everyone else, and it is Mrs. Devi. Now, go quickly and wash your feet properly. You cannot go with dirty toenails. And don't forget to take your quilt with you."

It was my first ride in an automobile. The man who drove the car sat in front, and Mrs. Devi and I in the back. There seemed to be a cool breeze trapped inside the car.

Amazed, I could not help asking, "Where does the coolness come from?"

"That's the air-conditioning in the car," Mrs. Devi replied.

Of course I had heard of such a thing. I could feel the cool air as I walked by the entrances of the more expensive cinemas, but here I was in the middle of it. Mrs. Devi talked pleasantly while I sat straight up, afraid to open my mouth. We drove though the streets, sitting upon soft cushions with our windows shut against the heat and dust. The people on the street seemed very far away from us. I thought of Raji and how hard he had to work to carry someone in his bicycle rickshaw and how easily the thing inside the automobile pulled us or pushed us; I did not know which.

Mrs. Devi said, "When I first saw your quilt, Koly, I thought of my baap. He came from a village very like yours."

I must have shown my surprise, for she went on to say, "When my baap was ten years old, his mother, who was a widow, was taken ill and could no longer work. Baap was sent to stay with his uncle for a few days. When he returned, he found that his maa was gone. He was told she had died, but he soon found out she had been taken to Vrindavan and abandoned here."

I stared at Mrs. Devi, amazed at the telling of this story, which was so much like my story. "What happened?" I whispered.

"The unhappy boy ran away to Vrindavan to find his maa. He got a job as a helper to an iron-monger. At the end of each day he looked for his maa, but he never found her. One day a man who made his living drilling wells for water came to have his drill repaired. My baap, who was now a young man, had an idea that if the drill were made in a certain way, it would be more effective. And so it was. He began to make such drills, and soon they were sold all over India, and he became rich." She smiled at me. "When he died, he left money in his will for a widows' house."

I had a million questions I wanted to ask, but the car had pulled up in front of a small shop. Draped in the window of the shop was a rainbow of saris. A small sign with the proprietor's name, Mr. Das, was in a corner of the window.

When we entered, Mr. Das folded his hands and bowed to Mrs. Devi. I liked the man at once, for he reminded me of the bandicoot under the veranda. He was sleek, with sharp black eyes and little ears. He was as quick as the bandicoot as well, for as soon as we had stepped in, he latched the door behind us, as if he had caught us and had no mind to let us go. I would not have been surprised to see a long tail snapping back and forth behind him. He greeted Mrs. Devi with a happy, expectant smile.

"No, no, Mr. Das, I didn't come to buy today. I came to bring you a gift."

He looked even more pleased.

"Here she is." Mr. Das stared at me. I am sure he knew at once from my appearance that I was not there to buy a sari of king's muslin. Still, he bowed to me and waited.

Mrs. Devi spread open my quilt. I wanted to disappear; I had looked around the shop, and the embroidery on the saris was very fine. I was sure it was beyond anything I could do.

Mr. Das bent over the quilt, taking a corner up in his hand and holding it close to his eyes. He turned the work over, and I silently thanked my maa for teaching me that one side must look as well done as the other. He nodded as if the quilt were something of value that had been dropped upon his path.

"That is Koly's doing," Mrs. Devi said. "She is looking for work, and why should she not work here for you? Could she find a more suitable place?"

Mr. Das's quick black eyes darted from the quilt to me and back. He did not seem anxious to have me, but I could see he did not want to displease his good customer. "There would be much to teach her."

"Could she find a better teacher than you?"

He looked at me again. "We might try," he said.

"Excellent! There is no time like the present. I'll just leave her here." With that she bowed briefly to Mr. Das, who hastened to return her bow. In a moment she was gone, and Mr. Das and I were left facing one another.

I couldn't help saying in a small voice, "You don't have to take me." I edged toward the door.

Mr. Das seemed pleased with my remark. "At

least you do not push your way in because of Mrs. Devi. Come with me."

I hurried along behind him. He led me through a long, dark passage that was more tunnel than hallway. At last we came into a large, bright room with five or six women sitting cross-legged, some on the floor, some on charpoys, all bent over lengths of cloth that were spread out over the floor like bright carpets. Around them were skeins of thread, scissors, and little fabric squares poked full of needles.

The women paused in their work and glanced at me curiously. They were all older than I, and I was sure that they did not think I could even draw a thread through a needle. Mr. Das hunted about until he came upon a scrap of cloth. He tossed it to me. "Show me what you can do with this," he said.

I looked quickly at the borders the other women were embroidering. One of the women was working a pattern of twining ivy. I did the same.

When Mr. Das came to look at my work, he shook his head. "No," he said. "Why should you copy what another does? That already exists. I want to see what is in your own mind." I expected him to send me away. Instead he gave me another scrap of cloth.

Raji was never far from my thoughts. Over and over again I had looked back at our evening at the river and wondered why I had not heard from him. As I thought of the river, I remembered the heron. I began to stitch its long neck and its head with its sharp beak. I stitched the long dangling legs and the great wings. I forgot where I was. From time to time Mr. Das looked over my shoulder but said nothing. When at last I finished the heron, I looked up to see Mr. Das standing there smiling. "That is what I want. It is not just a heron; it is *your* heron. It has flown right out of your head and, more important, out of your heart. Come back tomorrow, and I will have a sari for you to work on. I must think a little what weave and what color will be best. Now I suppose you want to know what I will pay you."

He named a sum three times what I was paid for the stringing of marigolds. Surprised, I almost told him the sum was too much, but one of the other women came up to him just then to ask for thread the color of the fruit of a mango. By the time he had turned back to me, I had resolved to hold my tongue. I smiled politely and said the sum seemed very fair and I would return the next day at whatever hour he wished.

Mr. Das's workroom became the most important place in my life. I couldn't believe that someone was paying me for doing what I loved best. There were days when Mr. Das looked at my work and shook his head. "Koly, what can you be thinking of? What woman would wish to wear a sari on which a dog chases a goose? You have lost your senses." So I put aside the memory of the little pariah dog and the gosling. I was able to embroider many other memories, though. I worked a design of silver hoops, and in that way I got my earrings back again. I made a pattern of marigold garlands in honor of Hari and to remind me of the hours I had spent in stringing the orange flowers. One thing after another in my life was captured and stitched to be saved. All the work was done on the finest muslin, each weave of muslin with its own name: woven air, dragonfly wing, summer cloud, evening dew.

My only sadness was Raji's absence. Each evening I waited in the courtyard hoping he would appear, hungry and eager to open a book. Each evening I was disappointed. At last I had to admit to myself that he had probably returned to his village and was looking for a suitable bride. Still, I could not keep myself from hoping I would see him again.

Sitting beside them each day in the workroom, I got to know the other women, who soon became my friends. The surprise was that they did not judge me by my age, but by my work. The older women laughed at some of my designs, but their laughter was kind. "Your designs are so original, they surprise us," one of them explained.

In the workshop scarfs and cushions as well as saris were embroidered. One woman kept a critical eye on my work and the work of the others. She always noticed when our threads became tangled or work had to be ripped out and done over. If we used too much thread, she reported it to Mr. Das. Because of her long sharp nose, which she was always sticking into the business of the other women, she was called the Shrew.

The Shrew shook her head over my work. "Who will buy such a sari? Women want what they are used to, not some outlandish thing."

"No, no," Mr. Das said. "My ladies are always asking for something new and different." He was a good-tempered man and treated us all kindly. He took an interest in our lives and would give time off if a woman was wanted at home for a child or a husband's sickness. Some women were even allowed to do all their work at home.

Only once had I seen him angry. A phul-khana, a wedding veil of fine silk and embroidered in gold thread, disappeared overnight. The phul-khana was meant for the daughter of a wealthy customer, and Mr. Das could hardly stand still with frustration. The embroidery had been done by the Shrew. Though her words were harsh, her stitches were deftly done. The scarf with its gold and silver moon and stars had been admired by all of us. She was as furious as Mr. Das at its disappearance. Mr. Das put new locks on our doors and windows and began to pay an old man to watch the workroom at night.

I began to confide in one of the younger women. Mala was nineteen, only two years older than I was, but she looked older. She was tall and as slim as a bamboo shoot. Her eyes were heavily outlined with kohl. Her long, tapered fingers with their bright-red nails pulled the threads in and out, stitching designs so intricate and clever, they took my breath away. Young as she was, Mr. Das entrusted her with embroidering threads of real gold. The Shrew was jealous of Mala and complained to Mr. Das that Mala often arrived late in the morning.

When Mr. Das scolded Mala for her tardiness, Mala only laughed. "Don't lecture me, Mr. Das," she would say in a taunting voice. "Your competitor, Mr. Gupta, down the street, stops me every day to beg me to work for him." Mr. Das would grow silent, for he couldn't bear the thought of Mala's clever fingers at work on Mr. Gupta's saris.

Often a young man would be waiting to walk home with Mala, but sometimes Mala would let me walk home with her, for her room was not far from the widows' house.

When Mala heard I was living at Maa Kamala's she said, "I know the place. How can you stand that old woman? She won't let you out of her sight. It's worse than a prison. Come and spend a night with me and see how delicious freedom is." I should have objected to the way she spoke of Maa Kamala, but I was anxious to be Mala's friend. I longed to accept her invitation, for I had heard from the other women in the workshop that Mala's room was often crowded with artists and musicians.

When I asked permission of Maa Kamala, she was indignant. "I know all about Mala. Her room is no place for a young girl. Certainly you cannot spend the night there."

"Just for a few hours then? I won't spend the night."

"No! Not while you are under my roof."

For the first time, I was angry with Maa Kamala. After our evening meal I whispered my plan to Tanu. "I'll say we're going to the cinema together. I'll give you the money for your ticket," I told her, "and enough for two lemonades."

Tanu was as eager as I was to hear about Mala's place. "All right, but don't be late. I can't sit in the cinema forever."

I borrowed Tanu's lipstick and kohl, waiting until I was out of the house to apply them while Tanu held a small mirror for me. I left her buying her ticket for the movie and hurried quickly toward Mala's place.

It was only when I reached the narrow dark stairway that led to Mala's room that I dragged my feet. What would a girl like me from a small village have to say to such clever city people? I wished I were safely with Tanu in the dark cinema sipping lemonade.

It was the music that drew me. The sound drifted down the back stairway and pulled me up the stairs toward it.

The door to the room was open. After a minute or two I gathered my courage and stepped inside. There were a dozen people there, as many men as women. It was the first time I had ever been with such a mixed group. I thought how horrified my maa would have been to see me in this room where men and women mingled. In the middle of the room were two men, one playing a sitar and the other a tabla. The fingers of the sitar player traveled up and down the strings like clever mice. The tabla player followed the notes of the sitar like a shadow.

Mala came to welcome me, leading me into the room. One or two of the guests gave me a curious glance. Mala pulled me down beside her on a cushion and turned her attention to the players. I glanced hastily about the room. Most of the women were older than Mala; at least with their sophisticated hairdos and makeup they looked older. A few of them wore jeans and T-shirts instead of saris or salwars and kameezes. Except for the musicians, who wore kurta pajamas, the rest of the men were also in jeans and T-shirts. They were talking and laughing together, paying little attention to the music.

There were real paintings on the wall and a rug on the floor. There was a faint odor of incense and something else that smelled sweet. I could see that Mala had electricity; there were two lamps in the room. To soften their glare, veils had been thrown over the shades. One veil was a pale blue, and its puddle of light was turned into blue shadow. The veil on the other lamp cast a pattern of moons and stars onto the ceiling. I looked again. It was Mr. Das's missing phul-khana. There could not have been another like it.

"Mala," I whispered, "it's the wedding veil."

"Of course. I took it to get back at the Shrew. Don't look so shocked. You're such a baby. Besides, Mr. Das doesn't pay us half of what we're worth."

What would Mr. Das have said if he had seen me sitting in the room of the person who had stolen his phul-khana? Before I could get up to leave, Mala summoned a man to join us. "Here is a real artist for you to talk with," she said. "Kajal, here is Koly, fresh from a village." Mala left us to greet a girl who had just come into the room.

I did not see how I could run away without looking foolish. The artist, Kajal, was studying me. He had a catlike face with slanted eyes and a half smile. "I must paint you," he said, looking as though he wished not so much to paint me as to devour me.

I tried to move away from him, but he took my arm and held on to me. "Those are my paintings on the walls," he said. "What do you think of them?"

There was a scene of a dark forest with a tiger peering out from some trees. The tiger had the same half smile as Kajal, which made the man more frightening to me. I saw that he was no house cat to be tamed, but a malicious cat, even a dangerous one. The other painting was of Mala. Kajal had made her very beautiful. At the same time the expression on her face suggested that she and the artist shared an unpleasant secret. "I'll make you look as beautiful as Mala," he said. "You must come to my room on your day off."

"Oh, no," I said. "I couldn't." Go to the room of a man! Maa Kamala would be horrified.

He held on more tightly to my arm. "You are no longer in a village now," he said. "You are living in a city. You are with adults here. You must act like one. Have some bhang. It will relax you."

I shook my head. I had passed bhang shops in the city. I knew bhang was made from marijuana leaves. "I have to go," I said. "I'm already late."

"You haven't had anything to drink. Let me just get you something cool. Then you can leave. I can see you aren't happy here."

The music had stopped, and across the room I saw the sitar player watching us. He started across the room toward me, but Mala reached out and drew him away.

Kajal returned with a glass of lassi. The glass felt cool in my hands, and I smiled gratefully at Kajal. I drank the lassi down, anxious to get away. After a moment the room began to whirl, and I felt sick to my stomach. I saw the sitar player, an angry expression on his face, pulling away from Mala and hurrying toward me.

I was outside. It was dark. The sitar player was supporting me, and passersby were giving us curious looks. "Where do you live?"

"I live in Maa Kamala's widows' house, but I have to meet Tanu at the cinema around the corner. Who are you?"

"My name is Binu, and you are a very foolish girl. How did you get mixed up with that crowd?"

"I work with Mala. She asked me to come. Why am I so sick?"

"That animal, Kajal, was playing a trick on you. The lassi was laced with bhang. You're lucky I was there. The sooner I hand you over to your friend, the better. I'm not a nursemaid to take care of every naïve village girl."

As he propelled me toward the cinema, he grumbled, "You are no end of trouble."

I saw how foolish I had been. I had disobeyed Maa Kamala because I was excited about going to Mala's room. Now I hated Mala. I gritted my teeth and made fists of my hands trying to fight the tears. Little by little I began to calm down. "Why were you there?" I asked the sitar player.

"The boy playing the tabla invited me to come with him. It's my first time with that crowd, and the last. Here is the cinema. That must be your friend." With a sigh of relief he pushed me toward Tanu, who stood staring at us with wide eyes and an open mouth.

I turned to thank him, but he was hurrying across the street and didn't look back.

"What happened to you?" Tanu asked. "You look upset."

When I finally got all the story out, she said, "How can such wicked people be?"

We were nearly at the widows' house. I stopped, afraid to face Maa Kamala. Tanu brought out her bit of mirror. "Comb your hair and wipe off the makeup. The kohl has run down on your cheeks. I'll say something we ate in the cinema made you sick."

I was sure Maa Kamala would see at once all

that had happened and would make me leave the house.

"Let me do the talking," Tanu said. To a worried Maa Kamala she explained, "It's her stomach. It was the monkey nuts. We bought a whole paper full, and the greedy girl ate most of them."

Maa Kamala put her arm around me, and the kindness brought out my tears. "Poor girl, I'll fix some ginger water for you to sip. Then you must go to bed at once. If you're not better in the morning, I'll send a note to Mr. Das."

I nodded gratefully, sure that nothing in the world would ever make me face Mala again.

Yet in two days' time I was back at the workroom. I had a living to earn. Besides, even the thought of seeing Mala again could not keep me from my embroidery. On my first day back I would not look at Mala, but as soon as Mr. Das was out of the room, Mala whispered in my ear, "If you say anything about the veil, I'll tell your precious Maa Kamala you came to my house and took bhang." She gave me a sly smile. I moved hastily away from her, bending my head over my work so the Shrew, who was staring at us, would not see the look of anger on my face and become suspicious. I thought I would never be done with scolding myself for my foolishness, but the next day Raji returned.

eleven

He was waiting for me when I left the workshop. I was so pleased to see him that with no thought for modesty I reached for his hand. "When did you get back?"

"Last night. I went to Mr. Govind's and Tanu sent me here. But I must return to my village very soon. I have to get the lentils planted in time for the rains next month."

No sooner had he returned than I was to lose him again. "What about your rickshaw job?" I asked, hoping that might keep him here for a bit.

"I'm all finished with rickshaws. Koly, let's go back to our place on the river. I want to talk to you."

I was surprised at his request, but pleased at

any chance to be with Raji. And he had called it "our place."

As we walked along, I thought how the city had changed for me. When I had first come, the city had been unwelcoming, even treacherous, but now I had found my place in it. I had my work and friends. Still, I was never so happy as I had been with Raji, and I could not help but be sad at how soon he would leave me.

It was the dry season. We could see the muddy cradle of the banks through which the river ran. We settled on a patch of grass, and taking off our sandals, we swung our feet into the brown water. Behind us the deserted temple looked shabby. In the gloominess I could not help remembering my evening at Mala's apartment and wondering what Raji would think of me if he knew of it.

Raji listened to my silence for a while and then said, "Something is troubling you."

I nodded, unable to get out my words. Just then a heron flew over us and drifted down to the river's edge. We stayed quiet to keep it there. I wondered if Raji, like me, was remembering the first time we had seen it. After it flew away, Raji said, "Why should we have secrets?"

The whole story of my evening at Mala's came out in a flood of words.

Raji did not say at once that it was all right or that I was very foolish. He only looked out at the Yamuna River, which minded its own business. After a bit he said, "I would like to meet that Kajal. I would stamp him to pieces like the scorpion he is. I'm glad you told me, but that is in the past. I came back to the city to talk to you about what is ahead. My uncle has decided to rent half my land. With his money I can fix up my house. A man from the government is showing me how to make my land more fertile. Already the wheat I planted has pushed up. I want you to come back with me to my village. You would like it there. We have all the things that please you."

Puzzled, I asked, "But what could I do in your village?"

Gazing down, Raji mumbled, "You would be my wife, of course."

I stared at him. I had never imagined such a

thing would be possible. I thought I must be dreaming. "But what of your family?" I managed to ask. "They wouldn't want you to marry a widow; such a marriage is inauspicious. And you own land. You would have no trouble finding a wife who would bring you a dowry."

Raji tore up some reeds and tossed them into the river. "I don't want to marry a handful of rupees. Can I come to my house at the end of a day in the fields and talk with rupees? Can I bring up my children with rupees for a mother to watch over them? My maa and baap lived in the same house, but no word passed between them except when my maa offered a second helping of rice to Baap or my baap said the eggplants were wormy. I want to talk to my wife. I can talk to you.

"I have no family but my uncle and aunt. Surely I can make up my own mind. Anyhow, I have told them about you." He grinned at me. "Besides, I have need to improve my reading, and no one in my family can read."

I smiled back, but no words came. I could only sit there looking out across the river. The setting sun was turning the water from brown to gold. The first streaks of evening lay against the sky like a purple border on a blue sari. I had never thought of marrying again. I had known that Raji would make a fine husband for some lucky girl, but I could hardly believe that he had chosen me or that his family would accept me.

"At first," Raji said, "we'd be poor, but I have fixed the house up so the rains can't get in, and we would grow all the food we need on our land. My crop of okra and lentils will bring in money. There's a well in the courtyard. If we have water and food and a roof over our heads, that is all we need."

I still had not found words, and Raji studied me. "Maybe I should not have spoken. Maybe you do not care for me."

I looked lovingly at Raji's strong shoulders and brown skin and his foolish wayward hair, which he had tried to slick down with coconut oil. "I do care for you. I missed you when you were away. I was in the courtyard every evening looking for you." He took my hand, and I did not pull it away. Had I not always been happy with Raji? I wanted to tell Raji yes, yes. But his asking had happened so quickly. And what of my embroidery at Mr. Das's place, and my friends at Maa Kamala's house? I could see myself in two places, with Raji and in Mr. Das's workroom, but I could not see myself in just one place. "How could I give up my work?" I asked Raji. "What would I do?"

"You'll have the house to care for and the marketing and cooking." In a voice so quiet I could hardly hear him, he added, "And I suppose there will be children." He ran his hand over his hair, ruffling what was already ruffled.

I could not forget my days with Sass. I saw myself once again sweeping a courtyard and carrying heavy jugs of water. Even without Sass the work would be hard, yet Raji and I would be there together. "I don't know, Raji," I managed to get out. "Perhaps we should wait a bit."

In a disappointed voice he said, "You want to stay here and go to more parties at your friend Mala's."

"I don't! I wish I hadn't told you."

"I'm sorry." He looked miserable. "How long

do you want to wait?"

I thought for a bit, trying to make out what this new life would be like. At last I said, "Not long." When I saw the hurt look on his face, I couldn't help asking, "If I don't come right away, would you find another wife?"

"I have found the wife I want." He pulled more reeds up until I thought that if we did not leave soon, there would be no reeds left along the Yamuna River.

"It's late," I said. "Maa Kamala will wonder where I am."

"But you don't say no."

I shook my head. "I don't say no. Give me a little time, Raji, and yes will come." The pulling up of the reeds stopped and Raji took my hand again. He had a mournful look on his face. I reached up and smoothed his hair. "It is only for a short time, and I'll write to you," I promised. "Will you write to me?"

With a slow smile he said, "If you don't treat my letters like a lesson and send them back with red marks."

Each week a letter came from Raji. Some letters were no more than a few sentences, but some went on for many pages to tell me how the blossoms had come out on the lentils and how the water from his well was sweet and good tasting.

In one letter Raji wrote that he had planted a tamarind tree in the courtyard. "It says in the Vedas, 'He who plants a tree will have his reward.' How soon will my reward come?"

Often he told me of the birds he had seen, the hawks and falcons and once an eagle. In the evenings there were fireflies in the courtyard, and he could hear the cries of the nightjars as they circled overhead. Because Raji was a farmer, every letter told of the weather.

In my replies to Raji I told him how often I thought of him. I hardly ever mentioned the weather, for there didn't seem to be much of it in the city. It was very hot or it wasn't. The seasons were hidden behind all the houses and the traffic on the streets. Tanu and I had moved out of the widows' house and now had a room of our own with only one small window and no courtyard. For us the weather had disappeared altogether.

We had left the widows' house shedding tears and clinging to Maa Kamala. "You are women now and must make room for other widows here," she gently chided us. "Only don't forget us." There were tears in her eyes as well.

As I saw the fearful looks of the widows who were to take our place, I realized how much things had changed for me. I had friends and a secure job, and now I had Raji. But if I married Raji, would I have to give up my friends? My work? I lay awake at night trying to sort it all out.

Tanu and I were proud of having our own place. We put pictures from old magazines on the wall and bought two charpoys and a small hot plate to cook on. The entrance to our building was off a narrow alley. Four families lived in our building, and we all shared a toilet and a faucet where we got our water and did our washing.

At first it was exciting to have a room of our own, but I soon tired of it. It was the beginning of

May, and it seemed the monsoon would never come. There was no breath of air. Dust from the street covered everything. If I took my eyes from them, the walls of our room crept closer and closer to me until I thought I would suffocate. I could go up onto the roof, but the corrugated tin burned my feet. In the street there were a hundred other people breathing in the air I needed. There were no nightjars or fireflies or hawks to be seen. I began to long for Raji and his village.

I eagerly awaited his letters. The tamarind tree was doing well and one day would shade the courtyard. He had made shutters to keep out the rains when they came, and he was working on a surprise for me. Tanu teased me. "You will wear the letters out with all the folding and unfolding."

At the workroom tempers were short because of the heat. There were arguments over the sharing of scissors or who was to have the place with the best light. Even the sheerest muslin lay hot and heavy on our laps. Mr. Das said we were behind schedule, and his customers were complaining. He was always scolding Mala, who was coming in later and later. She only tossed her head and spoke of how Mr. Gupta was after her to work for him.

It was on a day so hot that we had to wipe our sweaty hands on a cloth to keep them from soiling our work that Mala was fired.

One of the women was embroidering a wedding sari, coiling gold thread along its borders and fastening it with the tiniest stitches imaginable.

"You haven't given me enough gold thread to finish the sari," she complained to Mr. Das. All the gold thread was kept locked in a cupboard. Only Mr. Das had the key.

Mr. Das looked puzzled. "Yes, yes. You are mistaken. I put a new skein beside you only an hour ago. You have mislaid the thread," he insisted. "That is no way to treat something so valuable. It must be somewhere. Look carefully."

The woman stood up and shook out her clothes and the sari she was working on. In a puzzled voice she said, "There is no thread here."

The Shrew was watching. She said, "Look in

Mala's purse." There was a satisfied smirk on her face.

We all looked at Mala. She snatched at her purse, but before she could reach it, Mr. Das had it in his hand and was opening it. Mala sprang at him, shrieking that he had no business with her property. As she grabbed the purse, the skein of gold thread fell out. No one made a sound.

"You are finished here," Mr. Das said, breaking the silence. "Go and work for Gupta. It will bring him nothing but trouble."

I was angry with Mala and disgusted with her stealing. Yet a part of me was sorry for her. All her beauty and cleverness were wasted. What had happened to her was like the breaking of a fine vase.

That evening, to forget the scene with Mala, I convinced Tanu to walk down to the river where Raji and I had gone. I was missing Raji more each day and thought seeing the river would bring him closer.

As I had hoped, the thoughts of Mala began to fade. But Tanu was a city girl, and all the open space around the river made her nervous, so we soon returned to our little room. A part of me returned, but much of me stayed with the river and the kingfisher and the heron and the memories of my times there with Raji.

In June a letter came from Raji with wonderful news. "My surprise is finished," he wrote. "I have built a little room in the house you can keep just for your embroidering. It has two big windows so you have the sun up and down. From one window you will see the courtyard and the tamarind tree. From the other window you will see the fields where I work."

It was not only the room that brought tears to my eyes but the idea of a room for me taking shape in Raji's mind, and then being built with his hands. My last doubts about the marriage flew from me like a flock of birds starting up from a field to be lost in the distance.

I thought often of the room Raji had built for me. There would be no sound of automobiles or motorcycles or buses. Instead, I would hear the rustle of the leaves of the tamarind tree and the sound of the birds that nested there. I would put up white muslin curtains that would flutter when the breezes blew across the fields. My son would be in the fields helping Raji. My daughter would sit beside me in the room, a small scrap of cloth and a needle and thread in her hand.

Once again I began a quilt for my dowry. My first quilt was stitched as I worried about my marriage to Hari, the second in sorrow at Hari's death. Chandra's quilt was stitched to celebrate her happiness. This time as I embroidered, I thought only of my own joy. "When it's finished," I wrote Raji, "we'll be married." In the middle of the quilt, spreading its branches in all directions, I put a tamarind tree to remind me of the tree in my maa and baap's courtyard and the tree in the home I was going to. I stitched Mr. Das, Mrs. Devi, Maa Kamala, and Tanu. There was even a place on the quilt for Mala, though I had heard she was no longer at Mr. Gupta's. I stitched a rickshaw and Raji in the fields and me embroidering in the room

Raji had made for me. Around the quilt for a border I put the Yamuna River, with reeds and herons beside it.

One day I confided my plans to Mr. Das. I knew there were women who sent their work in to him and hoped I might do the same. At first Mr. Das was distressed at my news, but soon his black eyes flashed with excitement.

"Why should you not be happy with your husband and home?" he said. "I remember the boy waiting for you outside the store. Very polite boy. Full of energy. I could tell that from the way he paced back and forth. With such a husband you will never go hungry. But Koly, you must not stop your work. Does he understand that?"

I told Mr. Das about the room Raji had built for me.

"Ah, that is good. Every few months you will come to see me, and I will give you work to take back to your room. But will you not have a house to care for? Meals to cook? Children whining for this or that? Will you have time for the work?"

"I'll make time," I promised. "The house will not always be so clean, the cooking may be a little hasty, and the whining children will sit on my lap and I'll sing to them while I work."

Mr. Das laughed. "If you make that a promise, I'll give you a sari for your dowry."

Tanu wasn't taking the news of my leaving so well. "You are lucky," she said, and her voice was bitter. "Where will I find a man who will marry a widow? And who will take your place here and pay so much rent?" Because I made more money than Tanu did, I paid a greater share. At Maa Kamala's place we learned of two girls who were looking for a room, and they were happy to join Tanu.

"Still, it won't be the same," Tanu said.

As much as I was looking forward to my marriage, I knew how much I would miss Tanu. "I'll see you when I bring my work to Mr. Das," I promised, "and you can come and visit us in the country."

Tanu shook her head. "I'll see you here, but you won't get me near the country. It's full of snakes."

The rains had come. In his letters Raji told how green everything was. He wrote proudly of how the government agent had brought other farmers to see how well his crops were doing. Sometimes, he said, he looked into the room he had built for me, hoping to see me there. How soon would the quilt be finished?

In my answer I wrote that the quilt was almost done. "No more than a week or so," I promised. More and more my thoughts flew to Raji, and I stayed up late in the evenings, finishing the quilt.

At Mr. Das's workshop we listened to the rain beat steadily on the tin roof. We were snug and comfortable in our workroom, teaching one another stitches, trading gossip, telling one another our plans. The workroom and the women in it had become a part of me. All the while I stitched, I thought of how lucky I had been to find Raji, and how without him my life would have been very different. Even in my happiness my thoughts sometimes wandered to Sass. I thought that because of her sharp tongue and unloving ways, she would not find a welcome in her brother's home. Poor Sass.

Mr. Das must have told Mrs. Devi that I was to be married. The next time she came to the store, she said to Mr. Das, "I must have the first sari Koly embroiders in her new home. You will give her a length of king's muslin to take with her." She smiled at me. "Koly, will you find something for the border in one of Tagore's poems?"

Immediately I knew that it would be the homeless bird, flying at last to its home.

author's note

Koly speaks Hindi, which is one of many languages spoken in India. Here are definitions of some of the words you will find in this book.

> *baap:* father.
> *bahus:* daughter-in-law.
> *bhagat:* a practitioner of folk medicine.
> *bhang:* leaves and flowers of the hemp plant.
> *Brahman:* the highest Hindu caste.
> *caste:* a social rank or division into which Hindu society is divided.
> *chapati:* unleavened bread baked on a griddle.
> *charpoy:* a wooden bed frame laced with rope.
> *choli:* a short-sleeved blouse worn under a sari.
> *chula:* a stove of baked clay sometimes with a tin oven.

dal (or *dhal*): a spiced sauce of pureed lentils.

darshan: experiencing a religious feeling by being exposed to a sacred object or place such as the Ganges River.

gataka: a person who arranges marriages.

ghat: wide steps usually leading down to a river.

ghee: butter that has been heated and had the milky substance poured off.

kameez: a long, loose shirt.

kautuka: a yellow woolen thread worn by a bride around her wrist.

kohl: a powder used as an eyeliner and to darken the eyebrows.

Krishna: a Hindu god.

kurta pajama: a long shirt and loose pants.

lassi: a drink made with yogurt and fruits and spices. Ice is often added.

maa: mother.

mantra: a word or phrase repeated or sung over and over, often as a religious devotion.

masala: a blend of spices such as cinnamon, saffron, cloves, peppercorns, and cumin ground together to flavor food.

namaskar: a greeting accompanied by holding the palms together at chest level to greet equals and at the forehead for someone who is greatly honored.

phul-khana: a traditional wedding veil.

poori: bread that has been fried in hot oil until it puffs. It's often stuffed with vegetables and spices.

puja: a Hindu ceremony of religious worship.

Rama: a Hindu god.

rupee: a unit of money; about 43 rupees are equal to today's American dollar.

sadhu: a holy man.

salwar: loose slacks.

samosa: a little turnover; samosas are made with a variety of fillings.

sari: a length of cloth, traditionally 6 meters, wrapped to make a skirt and then draped over the shoulder and the head.

sass: mother-in-law.

sassur: father-in-law.

shikanji: a drink of lime and ginger juice.

sitar: a stringed instrument.

tabla: a set of two drums.

tali: a tray.

tikka mark: a round vermilion mark painted on the forehead, symbol of the third eye of wisdom; also a kind of beauty mark.

The Vedas: the Hindu sacred writings.

wallah: a person who is in charge; often someone who has something for sale.

Rabindranath Tagore (1861–1941) was one of India's greatest poets. Tagore also wrote plays and stories, composed music, and worked for India's independence from Great Britain. In 1913 he received the Nobel Prize for literature.